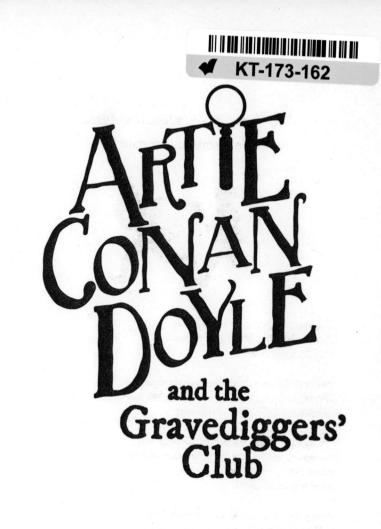

ARTIE CONAN DOYLE

and the Gravediggers' Club

ROBERT J. HARRIS

Kelpies

1.

The Adventure of the Haunted Graveyard

Edinburgh, January, 1872

As the winter's night fell, an icy sea fog crept over Leith then nosed its way up the narrow streets and alleyways of Old Edinburgh. It spread silently over Greyfriars Kirkyard, washing up against the walls of the church and coiling about the trees and gravestones. A distant clock struck ten as two figures, a pair of twelve-year-old boys, made their way cautiously through the murk.

"*Arthur Conan Doyle*," declared Artie Doyle. "That's what it will say on my tombstone, Ham, my full and proper name. And underneath that it will say, *He achieved greatness as… as…*"

"As what, Artie?" asked his friend Edward Hamilton.

"I don't know yet, Ham," Artie confessed. "That will take a bit of finding out."

Ham's green plaid jacket was buttoned right up to the neck, his shoulders hunched against the cold.

"I do wish you wouldn't talk about being dead." He tugged his cap down over his ears. "I've got goosebumps already just from sneaking around this graveyard."

Artie was also dressed for a winter's night in a tweed jacket, knee-length woollen trousers, long thick socks and a pair of stout leather boots. He tightened his scarf as he walked among the gravestones.

"Don't complain," he chided his friend. "Getting in here turned out to be easier than I thought, what with the lock on the gate being broken."

"A good thing too," said Ham. "I'd likely have ripped my britches climbing over it."

Artie stopped and rubbed his hands together. "Doesn't that broken lock suggest something to you?"

"It suggests to me that the watchman has been sleeping on the job."

"That's true, I suppose," Artie agreed. "But to me it suggests somebody wanted access to the kirkyard after hours. I wonder how long the lock has been broken."

"It may not mean anything." Ham jammed his hands deep into his pockets. "It might have been damaged by accident."

Artie frowned at his friend. "Look, there's no point sneaking out of the house in the middle of the night to have an adventure if you keep saying everything's an accident or a coincidence."

Ham gave a huff. "I'm sure I didn't mean to spoil it for you."

A shaft of moonlight suddenly pierced the drifting fog to illuminate a nearby gravestone. Artie bent down to examine the inscription.

THOMAS DOCHERTY
COAL MERCHANT

BORN 1757
DIED 1808

REQUIESCAT IN PACE

He straightened up and translated the three Latin words at the end. "Rest in peace." Artie paused thoughtfully. "Ham, do you never wonder what comes after – you know, beyond the grave?"

"I do not," Ham stated firmly. "I expect I'll find that out when the time comes and not before."

"Father Cassidy and the other priests at school talk about it quite a lot," said Artie. "But I don't see how they can really know."

"Well, you can take that up with them, if you please," said Ham. "Assuming we don't freeze to death right here."

Though both boys hailed from Edinburgh, they spent most of the year at Stonyhurst College, a boarding school in Lancashire run by Jesuit priests. They would have been back at school already if the roof of the east wing hadn't collapsed during a violent December storm, extending their Christmas holiday while repairs were made.

"Keep moving," Artie suggested. "That will warm you up. And keep your eyes peeled."

"Peeled? Peeled for what?"

"Well, ghosts for one thing. If we actually saw a ghost that would be proof, wouldn't it, that something lies beyond?"

Ham shuddered. "Listen, if we run into a ghost, you can ask him all the questions you want about what they do on the other side, what they have for tea and suchlike. Me – I'll be gone as fast as a hare with its tail on fire."

"You wouldn't just leave me here to face a ghost alone, would you?"

"I would," Ham answered flatly. "It's not like when I

helped you in that fight with the barrow boys. I doubt you can land a punch on a ghost."

"Well, if we can't harm them, it stands to reason that they can't hurt us either."

"Reason has nothing to do with it," Ham asserted firmly. "People have been running away from ghosts for hundreds of years and I don't intend to break with tradition."

Artie made an exasperated noise and walked on.

Ham hesitated for a moment, then followed. "Of course it might be different if it was a very small ghost, like that wee terrier that died last week."

"What, you mean Greyfriars Bobby?" said Artie. "The dog that used to sleep here?"

The little terrier was famous throughout Edinburgh and all the newspapers had reported his recent passing.

"That's right," said Ham. "He didn't leave his master's grave for these past fourteen years. Maybe his ghost is still haunting the place." He peered all around, as if expecting the little ghost dog to pop right up out of the ground.

"Don't you think that if he missed his master so badly, he'd hurry to join him in Heaven rather than hanging around this place?" Artie pointed out.

Just then Ham seized his forearm. Artie saw that his friend's eyes had grown wide with horror and when he followed Ham's gaze his own heartbeat quickened.

Through the sheets of fog he could just make out a figure

standing below the bare, skeletal branches of a hawthorn tree. He grabbed Ham by the shoulder and pulled him down behind the nearest gravestone. They crouched there, raising their heads just enough to peep over the top of the stone.

Shrouded in a grey hood and cloak, the apparition drifted slowly across the churchyard. No face could be seen beneath the shadow of the hood, but the two pale, slender hands clutching the cloak tightly in place gave Artie the impression that the spectre was female. Occasionally it paused by a grave before continuing its progress across the kirkyard.

"The Lady in Grey!" said Ham in a choked whisper. "They say she died a hundred years ago upon hearing the news that the man she loved had been killed in battle. Now she wanders the churchyards of Edinburgh searching for his grave."

As the cloaked figure drew closer, the two boys shrank down lower behind the gravestone. Keeping as still as stone themselves, they held their breath, counting the seconds as the eerie stranger drifted past. At last Artie dared a glimpse and caught sight of her fading into the fog. He stood up.

"Come on, let's follow."

Ham held back. "Let her go! For all we know, it might be a demon hiding under that hood."

"Come on!" urged Artie. "We don't want to lose her."

Even as he spoke, a fresh billow of fog rolled over them and the Lady in Grey disappeared in the gloom. Artie strained his eyes until they ached but could see no trace of the ghostly figure.

Turning to Ham, he saw his friend take a bite out of a currant bun.

"Where did that cake come from?" he demanded.

"I always have a cake in my pocket." Ham brushed crumbs from his collar. "You know, in case of emergencies."

"Emergencies?" Artie echoed. "I thought you said you ate cake when you were bored. Isn't this situation interesting enough for you?"

"I also eat when I'm frightened," said Ham, "and right now I am very, very frightened."

"Ham, I'm beginning to suspect that whatever mood you're in, it inclines you towards cake," said Artie crossly. He plucked the cake out of his friend's hand and tossed it away.

Ham stared dolefully after the bun as it rolled across the damp ground into the shadow of a tall, marble angel.

"I say, that's a bit much," he protested, "snatching a chap's cake."

"Ham, half the reason for bringing you along on this adventure was to break you of this cake habit."

"I still don't see why you wanted to come here," Ham said unhappily. "What is it you're looking for?"

Artie shuffled his feet uncertainly on the dank ground then said, "You know that shady character Benjamin Warren?"

11

"What, the medical student your mother took in as a lodger? I can't say I've ever noticed anything shady about him."

"You haven't observed him the way I have," said Artie darkly, "sneaking in and out of the house at all hours of the day and night, always acting as if he's got something to hide. This morning I saw his overcoat hanging in the hallway. And," he added dramatically, "there was something sticking out of the pocket."

Ham gaped. "What was it? A dagger? A pistol?"

"It was a piece of paper," said Artie.

"Oh." Ham's shoulders slumped in disappointment.

"I slipped it out and had a look at it, then put it back so he wouldn't know." Artie leaned towards his friend and spoke in a low, secretive voice. "It was a list of graveyards all over Edinburgh, and Greyfriars was at the top of the list. Now, if he's as innocent as you suppose, why would he make a list of graveyards?"

"So he's interested in graveyards," said Ham with a shrug. "That's nothing to get excited about. My Uncle Tully used to wander around Edinburgh visiting all the public statues. He even talked to some of them. His favourite was the statue of Charles II in Parliament Square because–"

"This is not the time or place to blether on about your uncle or Charles II," Artie interrupted brusquely. "I'm quite sure Warren is up to no good and it's somehow connected to this graveyard. Now come on!"

He started off through the fog with Ham trailing reluctantly behind.

Aarrooooooo!

Suddenly, from somewhere in the distance, they heard a terrible howling. It shook the winter air, like a cry of inhuman grief.

The two boys froze in their tracks.

"What was that?" Ham quavered, his round face turning white. "A wolf?"

Artie felt his own blood running cold. "There are no wolves in Scotland any more."

"Then it must have been some sort of a monster." Ham's voice cracked with fear. "I've had enough, Artie. I'm getting out of here. Now." He stumbled off in what he hoped was the direction of the gateway.

Artie had no mind to argue.

"It's this way," he said, hurrying after his friend and giving Ham's elbow a tug to steer him in the right direction.

"I really wish you hadn't thrown my bun away," Ham groaned. "I could do with a bit of comfort right now."

The words were no sooner out of his mouth than he tripped over a small grave marker and pitched forward to land flat on his face.

"Ham, are you all right?" cried Artie, kneeling down beside his friend.

Ham didn't speak. His eyes were fixed on a muddy patch of ground just beyond the end of his nose. Slowly he pushed himself up.

"Artie, look at this. Look!"

Artie leaned forward and squinted at the marks on the muddy ground. "It looks like an animal's passed this way," he gasped.

"Do you suppose..." Ham got to his feet and gazed nervously about him. "Do you suppose it was the ghost of Greyfriars Bobby?"

Artie shook his head in numb disbelief. "No terrier made these marks," he said breathlessly. "These are the footprints of a gigantic hound!"

2.

An Encounter in the Fog

The air in the graveyard seemed to turn even colder. It was shot through with a deep sense of menace, as if the drifting mist might harden about them and trap the boys where they stood. Shivering, Artie and Ham stared warily around.

"A gigantic hound," Ham repeated in a trembling voice. "I don't recall the Lady in Grey having a dog, but I suppose she might have."

"A ghost dog would hardly leave footprints," said Artie, trying his best to sound unafraid. "It would have to be solid to do that."

"That's not much comfort." Ham stared down at the huge paw marks. "Whatever made these must be a monster."

"I expect the howling we heard was the same beast."

"That's even less comfort," gulped Ham. "It sounded ravenously hungry."

Slowly they backed away from the paw prints, darting anxious glances through the fog, expecting at any moment to be pounced on by a slavering beast.

"Which way is the gate?" Ham asked nervously. "I'm all turned around."

Artie was far from sure, but he was determined to act like a leader.

"This way," he said and set off along the gravel path to their right.

As they made their way cautiously through the gloom, the tiniest sounds made them jump – a whisper of wind, the creak of a branch. Every time the fog billowed towards them they froze in their tracks, half-expecting a monster to jump out of it.

A large, dark shape now loomed ahead of them.

"What is it?" Ham wondered warily. "A tomb, I suppose, full of skeletons…"

"No, no," said Artie with a note of relief, "it's the church."

Silent and unlit, Greyfriars Kirk looked as black as obsidian in the gloom, but the sight of it was somehow encouraging. The two boys hurried towards it and pressed their hands against the damp stonework like survivors of a shipwreck clinging to a rocky shore.

"Maybe we could go inside and hide out there till morning," Ham muttered. "I don't think ghosts and monsters are allowed inside a church."

"It's all locked up for the night," said Artie. Just then his ears caught a new sound. "Shh!" he hissed.

Somewhere among the fog-shrouded tombstones, two men were speaking. It was impossible to make out the first man's muffled words, but his tone was one of complaint.

The other man's voice was clear and sharp. "Keep looking, damn you!" he snapped. "You'll get your share when we find it."

"Yes, sir," they heard the other man grunt.

Ham pressed himself against the stone wall, as if trying to work his way into the church by sheer force of will. "Artie, they must be pirates or cutthroats or something," he breathed. "No decent person would be abroad in a graveyard at this hour."

"Apart from us, you mean," whispered Artie, straining his ears to hear more. "At least they sound human."

Just then they heard a deep, bestial growl that could only have come from the throat of some huge animal.

"The hound!" choked Artie.

It sounded terrifyingly close.

"For heaven's sake, let's get out of here!" pleaded Ham.

Artie needed no persuading. Finding the church had given him his bearings. Seizing Ham by the sleeve, he pulled him down the path to their left. As soon as the gate came into sight they charged towards it. They barged through and left it swinging behind them as they staggered out into the street.

The pounding of their hearts eased as soon as they were clear of the graveyard. The comforting smell of boiled cabbage and the sound of drunken singing wafted from the open window of a nearby tavern. However rough those singers might be, at least they were alive.

Heaving sighs of relief, the boys left the Old Town and headed for the Southside where they both lived. The streets were quiet, with only the occasional horse-drawn cab or wagon rattling down the road. The gas-lit windows in the homes they passed were as cheering as candles on a Christmas tree.

Artie's spirits rose. "Well, Ham, we survived that adventure. And not only did we see a suspected ghost; we heard criminals at work, confirming my suspicions about Warren."

"Did either of those men sound like your lodger?"

"No, not really…"

"Then how do we know he's involved?"

"How do we know he's not? We can't prove anything by visiting just one of the graveyards on Warren's list. The next place was the Grange Cemetery. We'll go there tomorrow and search for more clues."

"So your plan then," said Ham glumly, "is to go on visiting graveyards until we're frightened to death by a ghost or devoured by some horrendous beast."

"My plan," said Artie firmly, "is that we be bold

18

investigators and find out what Warren is up to, not sit at home reading schoolbooks and stuffing our faces with cake."

Before Ham could respond, they were interrupted by the clomp of heavy boots, and a light came bobbing towards them out of the fog. As it drew closer, Artie saw it was a bull's-eye lamp attached to the leather belt of a police constable.

The constable was a tall man with a round head perched on top of a lanky body. He wore a black top hat and a long tailcoat. Halting in front of the boys, he unhooked the lantern from his belt and raised it high while he peered at them.

"Well, well, here's a fine pair of lads to be wandering about at this late hour. Lost, are we?"

"No, no, we're on our way home, in that direction." Artie pointed south.

"Yes, we're on our way home," Ham added anxiously, "so we won't trouble you any further Mr…"

"I am Constable George McCorkle." The policeman drew himself up to his full height. "And as a diligent guardian of the law, it is my duty to investigate anyone abroad at this hour, especially boys who should be in bed and resting up for school."

"We don't have school," Ham blurted out.

McCorkle's eyes narrowed suspiciously. "No school? Are you gypsies then? Or vagrants?"

"What my friend means," said Artie, "is that we do not attend school in Edinburgh. We are pupils of Stonyhurst College in Lancashire."

"That," McCorkle raised a questioning eyebrow, "is even more peculiar, for are we not well into the school term? And are you not many miles removed from Lancashire?"

"There was a storm," Ham explained. "Half the school fell down."

"Well, not quite half," said Artie. "But we can't go back for another week or so, when the repairs should be completed."

Constable McCorkle chewed on this for a moment. "Very well, but that does nothing to explain why you are hurrying down the street at this late hour of the night."

Faced with the stern might of the law, Ham fell into a panic.

"We're not doing anything," he blurted. "By all that's holy, nothing, I swear!"

"By all that's holy?" the constable repeated, intrigued. "That's a strong oath indeed."

Artie resisted the urge to clamp a hand over Ham's mouth to shut him up.

"What my friend means," he said, "is that we have been out on an errand delivering groceries to a sick relative, and we lost track of the time. Realising the lateness of the hour, we are hurrying home to spare our families any worry."

"Well, that's motive enough for haste," the constable allowed, "and a worthy task for honest young gentlemen."

His small brown eyes darted up and down as he scrutinized each of the boys in turn, then he stood for a moment, stroking his moustache. "You appear to be in possession neither of stolen property," he surmised, "nor harmful weapons. You are decently dressed and for the most part well spoken. From this I conclude that you are respectable citizens. You may proceed on your way."

"Thanks very much, sir," said Artie gratefully. But his relief was short lived.

Just as he and Ham started up the road, the constable stepped back into their path.

"Just a moment, if you please," he said. "As you are honest young gentlemen, I am sure you won't mind lending me some assistance with my inquiries."

"I really don't think we can be of any help." Artie tried to edge his way past.

"No, we're not very observant," Ham agreed, "and we don't have any contacts in the criminal underworld."

"I don't suppose you do," said the constable, with a twinkle of amusement in his eye. "However, you do appear to be coming from the direction of Greyfriars Kirkyard and there have been rum doings afoot in that area. I'm sure not much would slip past a pair of well-schooled young fellows like yourselves."

21

"I wouldn't be too sure of that," Ham mumbled.

"So, did you notice anything peculiar while passing the kirkyard?"

"Do you mean ghosts?" squealed Ham. "Or dogs? Or pirates? Or—"

Artie jabbed an elbow into his friend's ribs to stop the nervous flow of words pouring out of his mouth.

"What sort of thing do you mean, constable?" he asked in a business-like manner.

"Lights, perhaps," said the constable, "or perhaps some rough-looking knaves skulking about with shovels under their arms?" He raised both eyebrows to indicate the seriousness of the inquiry.

"What, do you mean gardeners?" said Artie innocently.

"I mean," said McCorkle grimly, "graverobbers."

3.

Drumbeats in the Night

"You haven't spotted any devious-looking scoundrels with shovels, have you?" inquired the constable.

Artie felt a chill run down his spine as he recalled the voices in the graveyard. If graves had been robbed and they admitted to being at Greyfriars at the time, he and Ham might find themselves accused of the crime.

"We definitely didn't see anybody with shovels," he answered truthfully.

"Or dead bodies," said Ham. "I say, they don't go around with corpses slung over their shoulders, do they?"

"Well, young gentlemen," McCorkle tapped a finger below his right eye, "you keep your eyes peeled, and if you have anything to report, ask for me at the Police Office."

"We will, sir," Artie promised. "And a very good night to you."

The policeman moved on. As his heavy footsteps faded into the fog, Ham asked Artie in a shocked tone, "Do you suppose those voices we heard might have been graverobbers?"

"They were definitely looking for something, so quite possibly," said Artie.

As they hurried through the foggy streets, now desperate to get home, Ham shuddered. "Ghosts. Graverobbers. Why on earth would anybody want to dig up a grave? I should think the smell is awful."

"Sometimes rich people have valuables buried in their coffins, so thieves dig them up searching for loot. Sometimes bodies are used in medical research – you know, to teach anatomy."

"Well that rules out a career in medicine as far as I'm concerned," said Ham.

"Years ago, right here in Edinburgh," said Artie, "those famous criminals Burke and Hare dug up graves and even murdered people so they could sell the bodies to unscrupulous doctors."

"Suppose there were graverobbers in Greyfriars tonight," Ham's voice trembled, "and they'd caught us snooping around. Why they might have…" His voice tailed off in dread.

Artie decided it was best to reassure his friend to stop him going into a panic. "The voices we heard were probably

24

watchmen. And the ghostly figure might have just been a grieving young woman."

"But if she was a ghost, Artie," Ham suggested uneasily, "it might be that someone dug up her grave, and that's why her restless spirit is roaming abroad. If I were dead and some bounder dug up my grave, I would be jolly cross, I can tell you."

"I don't think you'll ever be a wandering spirit," said Artie. "It's hard enough getting you out of bed, never mind stirring you out of the grave."

The flat expanse of the Meadows opened up before them and, after a final farewell, Ham veered aside to cover the last short distance to his home in Buccleuch Street. Artie carried on across the dark Meadows, leaving the path to take a shortcut through the damp grass.

On sunny days the Meadows was a happy park with children playing tig and football, and families laughing over their picnic of sandwiches and lemonade. But on this cold, dark night with fog shrouding the city on every side, Artie felt like he might be tramping across a barren moor or some deserted Highland glen.

For a moment his mind was filled with ancient tales of lost travellers being waylaid by fairies and never again returning to the friendly lights of the mortal world. Shaking such fancies out of his head, he pressed on until the fog became smudged by streetlamps and the yellow glow of tenement windows.

A few dimly lit streets brought him to the cul-de-sac of Sciennes Hill Place, where the fog had banked up so thickly he could barely see his way to the front door. Once inside, he climbed the narrow steps by the flickering light of a weak gas jet until he came to the third floor where the Doyle family had lived for the past five years.

He entered quietly so as not to wake his two younger sisters, who would be sound asleep by now. With luck his parents would also have gone to bed, leaving nobody to ask him what he was doing out so late. The hallway was dark, but a faint light filtered out of the half-open kitchen doorway. Artie approached silently and peeped through the gap.

Slouched in a wooden chair by the stove was his father, Charles Altamont Doyle. A plaid blanket was draped loosely about his shoulders and his nightcap sat askew on his head. His long white fingers were wrapped around a glass tumbler and on the table before him stood a bottle of inexpensive white wine with barely a glassful left at the bottom.

He tossed back the dregs of what was in his tumbler then reached out an unsteady hand for the bottle. Artie could tell at once that his father was in a melancholy mood, as he so often was during the dark months of winter. It was as though having no inner warmth of his own, his mood could only follow that of the seasons: happy in summer, gloomy in winter.

Just as Artie was thinking of sneaking off to bed, his father noticed him in the doorway. Charles Doyle blinked his red-rimmed eyes and stared hard at the boy, as if trying to make up his mind whether or not he was dreaming.

"Arthur, my boy," he said, his lips twitching in a thin smile as he waved his son forward. "You're home late." He paused and cast a doubtful glance at the window. "It is late, isn't it?"

"Yes, it is quite late," Artie admitted, stepping into the kitchen. The faint warmth emanating from the stove felt good after his long walk through the chilly night.

Charles Doyle's shoulders drooped, the exertion of a smile seemingly too much for him. "Been out on some errand?" he inquired drowsily.

"I was over at Edward Hamilton's, revising history and geography." In Artie's mind this wasn't entirely a lie. He had started out at Ham's, leafing through some schoolbooks, before dragging his friend along on their graveyard adventure. Surely it wasn't wrong to think of exploring the kirkyard as an exercise in history and geography. Perhaps it even counted towards religious studies.

"That is very conscientious," said his father, with an approving nod.

"Well," said Artie, "Father Colley told us we mustn't let our minds grow rusty during the enforced break and that constant study was the best way to keep our wits sharp."

"A sharp mind is a wonderful thing," his father murmured. "It's very cold out though."

"Yes, it is," Artie agreed. He warmed his hands in front of the stove while his father sipped at his drink.

"I find the winter is colder in the city than in the country," Charles Doyle observed, tugging the blanket more tightly around his thin shoulders. "Curious that, isn't it? You'd think the city would be warmer, what with all the bodies pressed together in these narrow streets."

Artie knew his father hadn't ventured out that day. He had absented himself from his job as a surveyor at the Office of Works, claiming he had taken a chill. Artie noted a few spots of paint on his father's hands, evidence that he had been attempting to complete one of his paintings.

"When I find success as an artist," Charles Doyle mumbled, "we shall move to the country, you, your mother, your sisters and myself. We shall go for boat rides on the river, we shall fish for... for..."

At that point his weary eyes closed and his head drooped until his chin was resting on his chest. He began to snore softly. Gently Artie removed the glass from his father's thin fingers and set it down on the table beside the empty bottle. He tucked the plaid blanket more snugly around the sleeping artist, then left quietly so as not to wake him.

It was much colder in Artie's own room. He struck a match and lit the small oil lamp on his bedside table, as much for the meagre heat as for the light. Pinned to the wall was a half-finished painting his father had given him of a

28

knight emerging from a cave, shielding his eyes against the brightness of the sun.

In a corner, invisible in the shadows, was a stack of schoolbooks, covering maths, geometry, history and Latin. Beside the small bed was a larger pile of books, which were more to Artie's liking: tales of adventure and suspense. On top of the pile was a copy of *The Legends of King Arthur*, the ancient king after whom Artie was named. It always fired his imagination with thoughts of noble quests and heroic battles.

Artie pulled out a chair and sat down at his desk. He opened his journal and turned to a new page.

The Case of the Greyfriars Graverobbers

List of graveyards found in the suspect's overcoat pocket:

Greyfriars
Grange
Dalry
Calton Burial Ground
Dean
Newington
Rosebank
Warriston

Greyfriars Kirkyard,
Thursday, January 18, 1872, 10.00 pm

Graverobberies in this location confirmed by Constable McCorkle.

Overheard two men's voices, searching for something. Heard the howl of, and saw footprints of, a gigantic hound. Saw a ghostly figure, possibly the legendary Lady in Grey.

Next course of action: investigate Grange Cemetery.

Artie put away his pen and inkpot, changed quickly into his nightshirt, keeping his thick woollen socks on, and jumped into bed. Burrowing down under the covers, he waited for his fingers to stop shivering, then pulled a book from under his pillow. It was *The Last of the Mohicans* by James Fenimore Cooper, an exciting tale of war in America. He flipped to the part he had reached last night, where, guided by the brave hunter Hawkeye, some British colonists were hiding in a cave from the fierce Huron warriors who pursued them. Only now, as he was reading, did tiredness catch up with him, and he dozed off.

Far down in his dreams, he too was concealed in a cave,

hiding from fierce enemies. Off in the distance he could hear the sound of war drums beating louder and louder as the ruthless foe drew closer.

All at once he started out of his sleep. It took a moment for him to realise that, although he was awake, he could still hear drumming from outside his window.

No, not drumbeats but rapid footsteps in the street below. Jumping out of bed, he pressed his nose to the glass and peered down at the gloomy cul-de-sac. By the dim glow of a nearby streetlamp he could just make out the figure of a man hurrying out of the fog, so pale and breathless he looked like he was being chased by the devil.

It was their lodger, Benjamin Warren.

4.

The Mystery of the Unwanted Lodger

The bedside lamp was flickering weakly. Artie snatched it up, annoyed that a lot of oil had burned off while he'd been dozing, and padded out into the narrow hallway. Holding the lamp aloft, he was just able to make out the face of the clock on the mantelpiece through the open parlour door. It was almost one o'clock in the morning.

What could Warren possibly be up to, skulking about at this time of night?

A few months ago his older sister Annette had been sent off to school in France, just as his mother had been when she was a girl. Artie had expected to move into her larger room. Instead, his mother had rented it out to this medical student.

"The extra money will be a great help to us," she explained to her disappointed son. "Also it will be a comfort to have a medical man in the house when there are so many winter ailments going round."

"Medical man?" Artie responded sceptically. "He's just a student."

"A student doctor," his mother insisted. "And every day he learns more and more of the healing arts."

The front door opened and the lodger stumbled in, panting from his rush up the stairs. He was careful to shut the door quietly behind him before facing the hallway. Seeing Artie, he gave a start.

"Oh, Artie, it's only you," he gasped, almost faint from relief. "For a moment I was afraid I'd seen a ghost."

Artie held the lamp under his chin, casting a sinister shadow over his face. "And why should anyone be haunting you, Mr Warren? Do you have something to be guilty about?"

"No, no, not at all," Warren responded, too quickly to be convincing. "It's just a manner of speaking, that's all. And do keep your voice down. We don't want to wake up the whole house, do we?"

"No we don't," Artie agreed in a rough whisper. "We don't want them to find out what you've been up to."

Warren frowned uncomfortably then forced a twisted smile. "You're joking, of course. And what are you up to, my fine lad, wandering about at this unholy hour?"

"I heard someone running in the street below. I thought it might be an escaped convict or a burglar on the run."

33

Warren gave a nervous chuckle. "Oh, Artie, what an imagination you have. You should be in your bed, dreaming about pirates and princesses." He brushed past Artie and opened the door to his room, casting a guilty glance back over his shoulder before disappearing inside.

Artie stood for a few moments, gazing at the door. There was no doubt in his mind that their lodger was concealing a sinister secret.

Following his long night out in the cold, Artie slept late and lay in bed even later, reluctant to leave the warmth of his covers. He heard his two younger sisters being ushered off to school, but only got up when the smell of fresh porridge wafted from the kitchen.

He dressed quickly and went in search of breakfast. His mother was standing over the stove stirring a pot of porridge. She licked the spoon then added a dash of milk.

"Up at last, eh?" she greeted her son as he sat down at the table, rubbing his eyes.

"I couldn't sleep for dreaming," said Artie.

"Well now, that makes no sense," said his mother with a twinkle in her blue eyes. "If you were dreaming you must have been sound asleep."

"Sometimes a dream is so vivid it wakes you up, don't you find?"

"Oh, when I dream, I just relax and enjoy it," said his mother. "Last night I dreamed I was in France, dancing through a vineyard under a summer sun."

"I was being chased by bloodthirsty enemies," said Artie. "I'm not sure if I escaped or not."

His mother laughed but before she could speak there came a sharp rap at the door. Wiping her hands on her apron, Mrs Mary Doyle scurried to answer it.

On the threshold stood a small, portly man in a grey tweed suit and bowler hat. Behind him Artie recognised the policeman he and Ham had encountered in the fog last night.

"I am Lieutenant Sneddon of the Edinburgh Constabulary," said the little man proudly, as if he were presenting himself as the Emperor of China.

McCorkle drew himself up to attention, waiting to be introduced, but Sneddon ignored him and continued in the same grandiose tone, "I am here to interview a resident of this domicile."

Artie's heart skipped a beat. Had McCorkle changed his mind about the two boys' innocence? Had he tracked down this address and summoned his superior? He quickly stepped back into the shadows of the parlour, where he could observe the visitors without being seen.

"By name," said Sneddon, "of Mr Benjamin Warren."

"Ben?" said Mary Doyle, taken aback. "Why, whatever could you want with him?"

"That, madam, is a police matter," Sneddon responded sharply.

The door to Warren's room opened and the student peered out. "Me? Are you looking for me?"

"If you are Mr Benjamin Warren of the Edinburgh School of Medicine, then I most certainly am. Might we have a word in private?" Sneddon glanced meaningfully at Artie and his mother.

With obvious reluctance, Warren backed into his room and the two policemen followed, closing the door behind them. At the same moment Charles Doyle appeared, looking bleary eyed and confused.

"Visitors?" he asked his wife. "Is it someone from the gallery about my request for an exhibition?"

"I'm afraid not, dear." Mary Doyle took him gently by the arm. "Callers for Dr Warren."

"*Mr* Warren," Artie corrected her. "He's not a doctor yet."

"Don't quibble, Arthur," Mary Doyle chided as she led her husband back to the bedroom.

Finding himself alone, Artie took the chance to press his ear to Warren's door. The voices were muffled and he could only make out a few words and phrases. Warren said something about being exhausted from his studies and Sneddon mentioned that he had been reprimanded for missing a number of classes.

The detective's voice abruptly grew sharper and more distinct as he inquired, "I would like to ask a few questions concerning your whereabouts last night."

Artie pressed his ear even harder to the door, not wanting to miss any of Warren's reply... until he was grabbed by the arm and jerked away.

"Arthur, this is not the behaviour of a gentleman," his mother scolded. "Spying on people!"

She dragged him roughly into the kitchen.

"Surely you want to know what's going on," Artie protested.

Mary Doyle pushed him down in a chair and stood before him with her fists on her hips. "It's no business of ours, I'm sure."

"But the police," Artie insisted. "Warren might be a thief, or a forger... or worse."

"Don't be absurd," said his mother scornfully. "Why should a doctor engage in any such shenanigans?"

"He's not a doctor," Artie asserted again.

"He's in training to be one, so he's a doctor *in potentia*, which is practically the same thing."

"If he's so innocent," said Artie, "why are the police looking for him?"

37

"The police often seek the assistance of medical men – to examine dead bodies for evidence and whatnot."

When Artie tried to speak again she pressed a stern finger to his lips to quiet him.

"I'll hear no more of this nonsense," she stated firmly. "Ben has been a great help to us. Why, when Lottie came down with that fever, she might not have pulled through without his care. And your father's seizure…" Her voice tailed off and Artie remembered Warren lifting the stricken Charles Doyle from the floor and carrying him to bed. He lowered his eyes, resentful of his mother's gratitude towards the interloper. Surely it was he – Artie – who should step up and act as the man of the house when his father was ill.

Mrs Doyle turned and saw the pot of porridge boiling over. "Oh good heavens!" she exclaimed. She grabbed a long wooden spoon and began stirring with furious concentration.

Artie spotted the two policemen emerging from the lodger's room. Warren paused in the doorway behind them, looking disturbed and pale.

"Now, mind and keep yourself available for future interviews," Sneddon cautioned him.

"Yes, yes, of course." Warren retreated into his room and closed the door.

Mrs Doyle was fully occupied with rescuing her endangered porridge and so did not notice Artie slipping out of the kitchen. He hurried to the front door and opened it a touch, so he could hear the two officers talking as they walked down the stairs.

"Medical men are a shifty bunch, McCorkle," Sneddon was saying. "I'll not trust any man that knows more about my own insides than I do."

"I'm sure you're right there, sir," McCorkle answered woodenly, as though this was a response he was compelled to give at least twenty times a day.

"Aye, it's a dark business with murky medical motives," Sneddon went on. "But mark my words, I've more than a shadow of a hint of a suspicion that the Gravediggers' Club is somewhere behind it all."

As the two men passed out into the street beyond his hearing, Artie stood in the doorway, frozen with excitement over what he'd just heard.

"The Gravediggers' Club," he repeated to himself under his breath. "They're behind it all."

He went back to his room and opened his journal. Taking up his pen, he amended the heading of the case to:

~~The Case of the Greyfriars Graverobbers~~
The Mystery of the Gravediggers' Club
List of graveyards found in the suspect's overcoat pocket:

Greyfriars

Interview with a
Gravedigger

"A club?" said Ham. "Why would gravediggers have a club? It's not like they're the jolliest fellows."

"Lots of people have clubs," said Artie. "Why shouldn't gravediggers have one?"

"I can't think their meetings would be much fun," said Ham. "Not unless there was plenty of lemonade and pudding."

They were seated at a table in Ham's front room later the same day. Ham lived with his mother, Mrs Lucinda Hamilton, who was giving a piano lesson to one of her pupils across the hallway. Ham's father had died a few years ago and it was difficult for her to make ends meet. The piano lesson wasn't going well. Artie stuck a finger in his right ear to block out the din of a ten-year-old girl murdering Beethoven's 'Moonlight Sonata'. With the other hand he flicked through the pages of that day's newspaper.

"I say, what are you doing with that paper?" said Ham. "You're making a proper mess of it."

"I'm looking for funerals," Artie answered distractedly, running his finger down a column of newsprint.

"I don't like funerals." Ham made a face. "I was at my cousin Colby's funeral last year. It rained, everybody was miserable, Uncle Ross and Aunt Bess got into a fight, and at the supper afterwards there was hardly anything to eat."

"Ah, here's the thing!" Artie exclaimed. He was so excited he even pulled his finger out of his ear.

"What are you so worked up about?"

"Listen to this." Artie started to read aloud from the paper.

OBITUARY

◆

Mr Hamish Gowrie will be buried at the Grange Cemetery on Saturday, January 20 at two o'clock in the afternoon. Friends and relatives of the deceased are cordially invited to attend.

"I'm sure that's very interesting," Ham yawned, "but what's it got to do with us? We're not his friends or his relatives."

"Don't you see?" said Artie. "For one, it's the next graveyard on Warren's list. And it means that somebody must be digging poor Mr Gowrie's grave in the morning. This is our chance to interview a gravedigger."

"I'm not sure I want to interview a gravedigger. They're probably not very sociable, what with hobnobbing with the dead and all."

"We are going to investigate this mystery!" Artie declared. "If our lodger Mr Benjamin Warren is involved, it is vital that I expose him so that my family aren't suspected of any wrongdoing – or put in danger. Or would you rather stay at home and eat cakes?"

Ham turned away guiltily. "Well, of course, when you put it like that, it's a lot better to be out solving mysteries. I suppose."

"Good," said Artie. "Because with all those buns, you're in danger of becoming stout." He buried his nose in the paper, searching for any other items of information that might bear upon the case.

Ham lowered his gaze and mumbled, "My mother says stoutness is becoming in a man."

Next morning, the boys set out together for the Grange Cemetery, which fortunately was in their own area of town. The trees and bushes were flecked with frost and the sky was dark with the threat of snowfall. When they reached the entrance to the graveyard Ham stopped and shook his head unhappily.

"Really, Artie, this obsession with graves is getting a bit unhealthy. If we must investigate your lodger, are there no other leads to follow? Does he have any less gruesome hobbies?"

"What kind of hobbies?" Artie fixed his friend with a hard stare.

"I don't know. You're the one who lives with him. Does he go fishing?"

"Fishing?" echoed Artie. Memories flashed through his mind of how he and his father used to fish for brown trout in the River Almond, back when Charles Doyle was healthy and full of life. It hurt to think those days might never return.

"I've seen no suggestion that Warren goes fishing, and I've never heard of a fishing-related scandal," Artie snapped.

"Shame, I would much prefer a day's fishing to a trip to a cemetery." Ham had not noticed his friend's irritation. "Just imagine the thrill of reeling in a really big fish and landing it."

"And I suppose once we'd caught this enormous fish we'd cook him and eat him," said Artie.

"Well, that goes without saying," Ham enthused. "Pan-fried, I think, with butter and parsley."

Artie couldn't help grinning. "Ham, it's no wonder you're named after a kind of food."

"Actually my name is Edward. It's only you and the other chaps at school that call me Ham."

"Well, we're not abandoning our investigation in order to fill your dinner plate," Artie insisted. "Now come on."

He led the way into the cemetery. Under the sullen sky it looked an unhappy place, with a chill breeze tossing dead leaves among the gravestones. It was strange in this setting to hear somebody singing a Rabbie Burns song.

> *"Oh! what is death but parting breath?*
> *On mony a bloody plain*
> *I've dared his face, and in this place*
> *I scorn him once again!"*

"Where's that coming from?" Ham wondered.

"This way." Artie followed the sound of the song.

Weaving among the tombstones, they caught sight of a figure standing up to his waist in a grave, tossing up lumps of dirt with his shovel. The shape of the grave was marked out with a wooden frame and on the far side was a large box, towards which most of the earth was flying.

The gravedigger was a grizzled, brawny man with rolled-up sleeves and a kerchief tied around his brow. He swung his shovel in time with the rhythm of his song.

> *"Now farewell light – thou sunshine bright,*
> *And all beneath the sky!*
> *May coward shame disdain his name,*
> *The wretch that dares not die!"*

"That must be hot work, even in cold weather." Artie hailed the man in a friendly voice.

The gravedigger stopped his singing and looked up. He planted his shovel in the earth and crossed his arms over the handle. "Aye, ye'll have guessed that from my beet-red face."

"Especially at this time of year," said Artie, "when the ground is frozen solid."

"It is that," said the gravedigger. "Are you two lads here to lend John Dalhousie a hand?"

"What? In digging a grave?" Ham squeaked.

"There's nothing to be afeart of," John Dalhousie assured him with a mocking grin. "There's nobody dead in here yet."

"Well, I don't know about digging," said Artie. "We're not really dressed for it. But I could offer you something to drink."

"Drink is it?" said the digger, his eyes lighting up. "A nip of whisky maybe? A drop of gin?"

"More refreshing than that," said Artie, pulling a bottle out of his pocket. "Ginger beer." He held it out to Dalhousie who grasped it in his large, muck-encrusted hand.

"Ginger beer you say? Well, I reckon that's better than no beer at all to a man with a thirst." He tugged out the stopper and took a swallow that made him grimace in distaste. "It's ower sweet for a grown man."

Artie reached out to take the bottle back but the gravedigger ignored him and tilted it upward into his mouth. He gulped the lot down in five or six huge glugs then smacked his lips and wiped the back of his hand across his mouth.

"Well," he declared, handing the bottle back, "it was better than vinegar or the slops out of the privy, so I thank you for it."

He took a grip on the shovel and prepared to resume his task.

"I was wondering…" Artie interrupted.

The digger's eyes swivelled up. "You was wondering what?"

"Well, if you and the other diggers – your brothers in the noble art of the spade – ever meet, you know, socially."

Dalhousie leaned on his shovel again and fixed a curious eye on the boys. "How do you mean exactly?"

"Well, whether you get together to exchange stories of the many interesting sights you must have seen."

"Interesting, eh?" Dalhousie paused for a moment then, darting his head forward said loudly, "Do you mean GHOSTS?"

Artie was so startled he had to stifle a yelp and Ham nearly fell over. As Dalhousie laughed, the boys pulled themselves together.

"I wasn't thinking about ghosts so much," said Artie.

"I say, you haven't seen any ghosts, have you?" Ham asked. There was a tremor in his voice as he glanced round the cemetery.

"It may be that I have and it may be that I haven't," the gravedigger responded mysteriously, "but I'll wager I could tell tales that would scare the breeks off you."

"What I was actually thinking," said Artie, "was that maybe you and your fellow diggers might get together to discuss the technical points of your craft. Say, the best kind of shovel or the difficulty of digging through clay."

"I dare say them topics has come up a time or two," Dalhousie conceded. "Grave topics, you might say." He chortled at his own joke.

"Exactly!" Artie felt he was making progress at last. "Isn't there some place where you meet to talk about such things?"

The digger rubbed his unshaven chin. "Well, sometimes, of an evening, Lucius Bream, myself and a few others do get together for a pot of light ale at the Rooster and Trumpet."

"The Rooster and Trumpet?" Ham echoed quizzically.

"Aye, the public house in the Grassmarket," said the gravedigger. "The beer's not the best, but it's cheap enough for my purse."

"So I suppose it's a sort of club," Artie probed, "for gravediggers."

"You could call it that if you was minded to," said Dalhousie in an offhand manner. Then his brow darkened suspiciously. "Why so curious about us gravediggers?"

Artie flinched. He couldn't let this man know that he suspected him and his friends of body-snatching.

"Oh, it's my friend Mr Hamilton." He grabbed Ham by the shoulder and pulled him forward. "He has a burning ambition to be a gravedigger."

Ham was about to deny the whole notion when he spotted how Artie was frowning at him and knew he had to play along.

"Oh, right, me, a gravedigger," he stammered unhappily.

Dalhousie stared at him sceptically. "So what was it inspired you with this ambition?"

Ham stared at the man blankly.

"Well, go on, Ham, tell him," Artie urged. "It was at school, wasn't it?"

"Er… yes. It was when we were studying Shakespeare's play *Hamlet*," Ham improvised hastily. "You know, there's that scene where the hero, Hamlet, has a conversation with a gravedigger."

Dalhouise gave a dry chuckle. "Aye, whenever I dig up a skull I pick it up and have a wee chat, saying those lines from the play: Alas, poor Yorick…"

"Yes, digging graves has become Ham's passion," said Artie. "He's even been practising in his own garden. Go on, Ham, show him." He gave his friend a nudge in the ribs.

"Yes, I'm frightfully keen," Ham agreed without much enthusiasm. He mimed grabbing hold of a shovel and digging in the ground.

The gravedigger eyed him critically. "Your technique is badly lacking. You need to get your back into it."

Ham made his digging more vigorous, swinging his arms up and down until he was exhausted. Finally he laid down his imaginary shovel and stood panting.

Dalhousie shook his head. "You're maybe better suited to some other line of work. A cobbler maybe, or a baker."

Grrrrrrowf! Woof! Woof!

At that moment a wild barking sounded across the cemetery and a chill of fear ran down Artie's spine.

"The hound!" Ham squeaked. He was so startled he lost his balance and Artie had to catch him before he fell into the open grave.

49

"That's nothing to be frighted of," laughed Dalhousie, pointing to a yelping corgi darting among the headstones, trailing its leash behind it.

An elderly lady was running unsteadily after it crying, "Come back, Hamish! Naughty boy! Naughty boy!"

As the woman and her errant dog disappeared behind a marble monument, Artie and Ham tried to shake off the embarrassment of being so easily scared.

"Thank you very much for your advice, sir," said Artie.

"Aye, I need to get back to my digging." Dalhousie grabbed hold of his shovel. "You two had best stand clear or risk a face full of dirt."

"Yes, sir, and thank you very much," said Ham as the earth started to fly.

The two boys walked briskly away and, as soon as they were out of Dalhousie's hearing, Artie grabbed his friend by the arm. "Did you hear that, Ham? He as good as confessed to being a member of the Gravediggers' Club."

"To be fair, Artie, he was only talking about having a drink with some friends. You're the one that called it a club."

"And now we know where they meet," Artie enthused, ignoring Ham's scepticism, "the Rooster and Trumpet. All we have to do now is work out a way to spy on them."

"Artie, we're just schoolboys," Ham quailed. "We can't go poking around a public house. It's a place of drunkenness and thievery and heaven knows what goings on." He swallowed hard.

"It's true they might not let us in," Artie admitted, "and if we were spotted sneaking around, there's no doubt we'd be roughly handled. We need the help of a grown-up to investigate the place."

"Good luck finding one," said Ham. "I don't know anybody who would march into a den of criminal gravediggers."

"You're forgetting, Ham, that we've already met such a man," Artie reminded him. "Constable George McCorkle."

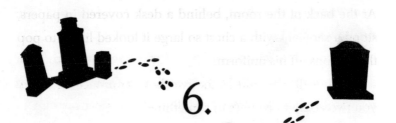

6.

The Return of
the Stolen Dead

By the time they reached the Police Office a few flakes of snow had begun to fall. The building loomed over them just off the High Street, at the top of Old Fishmarket Close, which the locals referred to as 'Poalis Office Close'.

In spite of the weather, Ham held back as Artie walked up to the door. "Do we have to go in there, Artie?" he complained. "Could we not just stay outside and wait for the constable to pass by?"

"We don't have time for that," said Artie. "Besides, it's too cold to stand around in the street."

"I suppose so," Ham sighed. He shoved his hands in his pockets and followed Artie inside.

Beyond a double set of wooden doors was a room where several greatcoats hung from pegs on the wall and descriptions of various wanted criminals were pinned to a notice board.

At the back of the room, behind a desk covered in papers, stood a sergeant with a chest so large it looked likely to pop the buttons off his uniform.

"Well, well," he said as the two boys approached, "have you two come to confess to something?"

Ham started at the suggestion but Artie smiled, realising it was a joke.

"Not at all, sir," he said. "We're looking for Constable George McCorkle."

Ham nodded his mute agreement. He shuffled his feet uneasily with one eye on the exit, as though he feared the sergeant might take a sudden impulse to toss him in a cell.

"McCorkle, you say," repeated the sergeant. "And what business have you with him?"

"He told us to contact him if we had any information regarding a certain matter," Artie explained.

Ham bobbed his head to confirm that this was the truth. At the same time he took a small backward step in the direction of the door.

"Well, McCorkle is out on patrol, as a good officer should be."

"Of course," said Artie. "Could you possibly tell us where we might find him?"

"At this time of day?" The sergeant glanced up at the wall clock. He drummed his fingers on the counter as he performed a brisk mental calculation. "I should say that if you lads were to set out at an energetic pace, you might well intercept him at the east end of Victoria Street."

"Victoria Street," Artie repeated. "Thank you very much, sir."

Once they were outside, Ham let out a huge sigh of relief, as if he'd been holding his breath for the last few minutes.

"For heaven's sake, Ham. Look what a state you've got yourself into."

"Artie, a chap's not safe among all those policemen. They're always on the lookout for somebody to arrest, and once they've got their hands on you, they'll find a way to make you guilty. Next thing you know, you're on your way to one of those convict colonies in Australia."

"I don't think they send convicts there any more." Artie turned up his collar as the snow grew heavier and strode off in the direction of Victoria Street. "Although I believe Australia is quite hot at this time of year."

"Could we not go home and wait there till it stops snowing?" Ham suggested, struggling to keep up.

Artie shook his head and lowered his voice. "Listen closely, Ham. I believe I've established what's going on. The gravediggers have formed a club in order to make some extra – and highly illegal – money. They know where all the best bodies are buried. They are digging them up and taking them to Mr Benjamin Warren. He is acting as their agent, selling the bodies on to medical researchers in exchange for a share of the profits."

"But, Artie, he lives in your house," Ham objected. "Where could he possibly keep all those bodies? Under his bed?"

"He probably has a secret cellar somewhere in town," said Artie darkly. "In crime stories the villain always has a secret cellar somewhere."

"Frankly, Artie," Ham made a disgruntled face, "I think you read too many stories. All that made-up nonsense is swirling about in your head getting mixed up with real things. That's why you keep chasing after these fantastic ideas."

"What you're missing, Ham, is that real life is often just as extraordinary as any story," Artie replied with an excited glint in his eye, "and it's good to be prepared."

"Prepared?" echoed Ham. "How do you mean?"

"Well, for example, I recently read a story in which the hero was captured by cannibals."

"And what did you learn from that?"

"That it's best to be captured by cannibals shortly before an eclipse," Artie explained. "You pretend to cause the eclipse through some sort of magic, and the cannibals will think you're a god."

"It sounds like it takes very fine timing," said Ham, "and rather a lot of luck."

55

"That's just one example. The general point holds true: stories give you tricks and plans to deal with all sorts of situations."

Once they reached the east end of Victoria Street they only had a few minutes' wait before Constable McCorkle came into view. He tipped his top hat to a pair of ladies dressed in furs then spotted the two boys.

"Well, well," he greeted them. "I seem to be running into you young gentlemen all over town. A proper pair of nomads you are."

"Actually, we were looking for you," said Artie.

"Looking for me? Not in any trouble are you?"

"No, but we have some information to report."

"Well, information is always valuable and that's the truth." McCorkle pulled out a pocket watch and squinted at it. "I'm on my way to lunch but I can spare you a few minutes while we walk."

As they headed down the street the constable shortened his lanky stride so the boys could keep up. Artie poured out his report while Ham slipped a pastry out of his pocket and began to nibble on it. Once he had heard about the interview with Dalhousie and Artie's suspicions of Benjamin Warren, McCorkle stroked his moustache meditatively before speaking.

"It appears to me, young sir," he began, "that you don't have the correct frame of mind for police work, if you don't mind my saying so. Too few facts and too much imagination."

Artie was affronted, and when Ham nodded in agreement with the constable he gave him a thump on the arm.

"I could make an excellent policeman," he protested. "If you like, I could follow Warren and find out where he's taking the bodies."

McCorkle held up a hand to silence him. "No need for that. It is true that we did interview Mr Warren and a number of other medical students about this matter. However, all that is irrelevant now."

"What do you mean?" asked Artie.

"A number of corpses, recently disinterred, were found in a hollow at Blackford Quarry early this morning."

Hamwas so aghast he paused in mid-bite. "Are you saying the bodies were just thrown away like rubbish?"

"So it appears. They were partially hidden but it was a poor job of concealment."

"And they are definitely the ones that were recently stolen?" Artie persisted.

"As well as that can be established, yes."

Artie and Ham exchanged puzzled looks. Ham shrugged and munched on his pastry, ignoring Artie's disapproving expression.

"I don't suppose it looked like medical experiments had been performed on any of them?" asked Artie.

"Not according to my information, no," the constable replied. "The police surgeon declares that they are all entirely intact. To be frank, the notion of the corpses being stolen for medical research appears to be a dead end, or, as we in the business call it, a red herring."

7.

The Puzzle of the Six Names

As he swallowed the last of his pastry, the smell of roasting chestnuts made Ham pause. They were now approaching the Grassmarket, where a man was selling the delicious treats from a cart, using tongs to pop them into paper bags for his customers. Pulling himself away, Ham hurried after Artie and the constable while the seller's voice echoed after him.

"Cheeestnuuts! Hot cheeeestnuuts here!"

Artie was clenching his fists in exasperation as he marched along beside the policeman.

"This makes no sense," he burst out. "Why would anybody go to the trouble of digging up bodies just to throw them away?"

"There seems to be little reason behind this crime," McCorkle admitted.

"But I overheard… I mean I thought I heard that the Gravediggers' Club was supposed to be behind it."

"That's as may be," said McCorkle stiffly, "but you'd do well to keep clear of those particular gentlemen."

"Gentlemen?" said Artie in surprise. "You mean the diggers who meet at the Rooster and Trumpet?"

"The Rooster and Trumpet? I'm afraid your information is erroneous on that score, my young friend," said McCorkle, as though correcting a small child. "I suggest you get back to your school work and leave the apprehension of dangerous criminals to me. Now that the missing bodies have been recovered, to all intents and purposes, this case which you are so agitated about is closed."

They headed down West Bow where a ragged musician was playing the fiddle in the hope that his jig would coax a few coins out of the passers by. McCorkle gave the man a stern look, as if to let him know that the law had an eye on him.

"So what's happened to the bodies?" Artie asked.

"Oh, they have been taken to the police mortuary," said McCorkle. "It is hoped that the deceased can be identified and returned to their graves, there to rest in peace, as they say."

He halted outside an eating house with a sign over the door showing a muscular arm flexing its bicep. Above the picture were the words 'The Lord's Arm' and below, in smaller letters, 'Truth, Virtue, Temperance'.

"This, young gentlemen, is a temperance house," the

policeman informed them, "meaning that no alcoholic beverages of any kind are served here, only sound, healthy fare. It is here I intend to take my lunch."

"Just a moment, please," Artie pressed him. "How are they going to identify the bodies?"

"Well, the doctor will ascertain what physical aspects remain and match them as best he can with the names on this list." McCorkle pulled out a crumpled sheet of paper and displayed it. "All six names are recorded here along with the cemetery from which each was taken."

"Could I have a look at that?" asked Artie.

"You can keep it." McCorkle handed the list over. "I have the names memorised, in case they should prove useful." He tapped his forefinger against his temple. "As I told you, I have the right sort of mind for police work. And now I will bid you good day."

With those words he disappeared inside the eating house. Ham watched him enviously. "I don't suppose we could go in there and get a bite to eat?"

Ignoring his friend's plea, Artie stared intently at the names on the list. "I don't understand this at all," he grumbled.

"It sounds to me like you've been reading the wrong stories, Artie."

"You needn't be so smug about it." Artie stuffed the piece of paper into his pocket. "Come on home with me and we'll give this some thought."

"There will be a warm fire there, I take it," said Ham hopefully. "And lunch?"

Half an hour later they were at the Doyle house and Artie was pacing back and forth across his room.

"If you're going to keep up this pacing, Artie, we could do with a larger room," Ham complained from where he sat, hunched up on the bed. "You're making me dizzy."

"I can't sit still when I'm chewing on a problem."

"I wish I had something to chew on," Ham muttered.

"We had those scones my mother baked," Artie reminded him, still marching across the room. "And you ate most of them."

"Oh, yes, those little scones," Ham recalled. "Those very little scones. You're going to wear out the carpet at this rate," he warned. "Besides, you heard McCorkle. The case is closed."

"How can it be closed when nobody knows who stole the bodies or why?" Artie protested.

"Well, there's nothing to be gained by fretting about it. Nobody cares except you."

"Read the names and cemeteries to me again," Artie instructed.

Ham flattened the list out on his knees, and read the names and associated graveyards aloud.

Donald Cafferty, Greyfriars Kirkyard

Charles Tennant, Greyfriars Kirkyard

Sidney Bruce, Dean Cemetery

Richard Chisholm, Dean Cemetery

Daisy O'Connor, Dalry Cemetery

Marie de Certeau, Dalry Cemetery

"There," said Ham as he finished reading. "Are you any the wiser yet?"

"There has to be some clue to this," Artie muttered, marching to the door and back to the window. He plucked the list from his friend's fingers and studied it. Then he dropped into a chair and pulled his journal from his pocket. Snatching up a pencil, he began scribbling.

"What on earth are you doing?" asked Ham.

"I'm comparing lists." Artie scrawled frantically in his journal.

~~The Case of the Greyfriars Graverobbers~~
The Mystery of the Gravediggers' Club

List of graveyards found in the suspect's overcoat pocket:

Greyfriars
Grange
Dalry
Calton Burial Ground
Dean
Newington
Rosebank
Warriston

"All the graveyards where bodies were dug up are on Warren's list!" yelped Artie, jumping to his feet. "Look, Greyfriars, Dalry and Dean Cemetery!"

"But half the graveyards in town were on that list, Artie. What does it prove?"

"Nothing – yet. But it confirms my suspicion that Warren is involved."

"You're pacing again," Ham noted unhappily.

Artie suddenly paused in mid-step, an excited gleam in his eye.

"Suppose," he suggested, "that the doctor who wanted those bodies wasn't planning to cut them up. Suppose he wanted to perform some other kind of experiment, one that left no traces for the police to see. And when he'd finished his work, he disposed of them."

"You really do have the most fantastic ideas, Artie," said Ham. "Next you'll be telling me that those corpses came to life and leapt into the quarry by themselves."

"Came back to life?" Artie repeated, his eyes growing wide. "Ham, you may have hit upon something there!"

"Oh no, Artie, you can't be serious," Ham protested.

Artie reached under his bed and pulled out a book. Excitedly he flipped through the pages until he found the passage he wanted. "Listen to this, Ham." He lowered his voice to a sinister solemnity and read aloud.

It was on a dreary night of November that I beheld the accomplishment of my toils. With an anxiety that almost amounted to agony, I collected the instruments of life around me, that I might infuse a spark of being into the lifeless thing that lay at my feet. It was already one in the morning; the rain pattered dismally against the panes, and my candle was nearly burnt out, when, by the glimmer of the half-extinguished light, I saw the dull yellow eye of the creature open; it breathed hard, and a convulsive motion agitated its limbs.

"What on earth was that all about?" asked Ham.

Artie showed him the cover of the book. "It's a novel called *Frankenstein* by Mary Shelley, about a doctor who brings a dead body to life using electricity."

"But that's just bosh," Ham snorted. "Nobody could actually do that."

"Don't be so sure." Artie put the book down and stared at his friend meaningfully. "I think I know a man who could."

8.

The Episode of the Dangerous Doorway

The next day was Sunday and Artie fidgeted so much during Mass at St Margaret's church that his mother had to give him three sharp jabs in the ribs to settle him down. Back home he squirmed restlessly as he sat with his sisters and parents, and gobbled down his plate of stewed beef and boiled potatoes.

"Is Mr Warren not joining us today?" his father wondered.

When the Doyle family returned from church, Benjamin Warren usually joined them for Sunday lunch.

"He offers his apologies," Mrs Doyle explained, "and says he will be absent on an errand of mercy for most of the day."

"Errand of mercy," Artie scoffed through a mouthful of potato.

"What was that, Arthur?" his mother demanded sharply.

Artie daren't mention his suspicions of what Warren was

really up to. He swallowed the potato and said, "Nothing. I'm just surprised he's working on a Sunday."

"The Lord himself healed the sick on the Sabbath," said his father. There was more colour in Charles Doyle's pale cheeks today, as if the short walk to church and back under a bright blue sky had done him some good.

"Quite correct," his wife agreed. She stared disapprovingly at Artie, who was wolfing down his food as fast as he could without choking. "What are you in such a hurry for?"

"Ham and I have a project we're working on today." Artie scooped up the last of the beef onto his fork and delivered it to his mouth.

"A project?" said Charles Doyle. "Might that also be deemed working on a Sunday?"

"Perhaps *you* should leave your school work alone today and set your mind on higher things," Mrs Doyle cautioned.

As he chewed, Artie tried to come up with a story that would satisfy both his parents. If they knew what he was really up to, they would probably keep him locked in his room until it was time to put him on the train back to Stonyhurst College.

"We're writing a history of the church," he said. "To go in the school library."

"A history of the church?" his father repeated. "That sounds ambitious."

"And unlikely." His mother raised her eyebrows.

"Well, it's a brief history, actually," Artie corrected himself. "But I'll be illustrating it with drawings of some famous saints."

Charles Doyle was delighted. "Really? You must show them to me when they're done."

"Of course," said Artie, rising from his chair. "I'd better get going. Ham will be wondering what's become of me."

"You will wait until everyone has finished," his mother informed him in a steely tone.

Artie sank back into his seat, as though pressed down by a huge weight. He rubbed his hands impatiently on his rough, woollen trousers as he watched the rest of the family eat with annoying slowness. His two sisters, Lottie and Connie, were dawdling their way through the meal and it felt like they might never finish. At last, when all the plates were cleared and Mr Doyle had said the traditional grace after meals, Artie was allowed to leave.

Artie arrived at Ham's house to find Mrs Hamilton forcing her son to practise scales on the piano. However, Ham's gratitude for the rescue was short lived.

"Let me get this clear," Ham said as they headed into town. "Your latest ridiculous idea is that your lodger stole the bodies to try to bring them back to life, then threw them in the quarry when he was finished."

"That's right," said Artie. "All I need to do now is to consult an expert on the matter."

"If you know a man who can raise the dead," Ham declared, "I most certainly do not want to meet him!"

"I never said Dr Harthill could raise the dead. He's an expert in medical science and electricity, so he will know if such a thing is possible. He will also know who could be performing such experiments, someone Warren might be in league with."

"That doesn't sound quite so bad," said Ham. "But I'm warning you, Artie, if we go in there to find corpses staggering around with sparks popping out of their eyes, you can fight them off yourself. I'll be gone before you can say Franklin Stone."

"Frankenstein," Artie corrected him.

"Well, whatever, I'll be gone in a flash. How did you meet this doctor chap anyway?"

"Last summer he advertised an electrical treatment he'd developed in The Scotsman newspaper. The advert said it could cure all manner of ailments so I went to visit him and we hit it off."

"What did you want to see a doctor for?" asked Ham. "You're not sick, are you?"

"Never mind about that," said Artie abruptly. "The point is, he's a very clever man who knows a lot about science, especially the power of electricity."

They arrived in Rutland Square, which, in keeping with the design of the New Town, was broad and spacious. At its centre was a private park with carefully tended lawns and tall, elegant trees, surrounded by orderly rows of terraced townhouses with large bright windows.

The boys climbed the four steps to Dr Harthill's shiny black door, which was flanked by a pair of Grecian-style pillars. The nameplate read:

DR WILLIAM HARTHILL
MEDICAL GALVANIST

Fixed to the door was a sign:

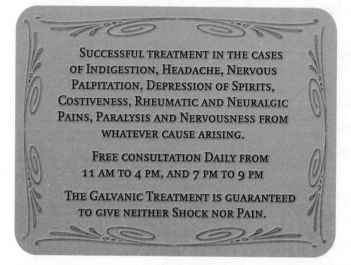

SUCCESSFUL TREATMENT IN THE CASES OF INDIGESTION, HEADACHE, NERVOUS PALPITATION, DEPRESSION OF SPIRITS, COSTIVENESS, RHEUMATIC AND NEURALGIC PAINS, PARALYSIS AND NERVOUSNESS FROM WHATEVER CAUSE ARISING.

FREE CONSULTATION DAILY FROM 11 AM TO 4 PM, AND 7 PM TO 9 PM

THE GALVANIC TREATMENT IS GUARANTEED TO GIVE NEITHER SHOCK NOR PAIN.

Artie rang the doorbell and waited for a reply.

After half a minute Ham let out a sigh of relief. "He must be out on his rounds. That's too bad. Let's be off home then."

Before he could take a step, Artie seized him by the arm. "He's probably just too busy to answer the door." He tentatively tried the handle of the door and found that it was unlocked. "Come on." He beckoned his friend inside.

"Artie, are you sure we should just walk in like this?" Ham worried.

"It's quite all right," Artie assured him. "I told you, the doctor and I are good friends."

The moment Artie stepped over the threshold into the hall there was a crash of breaking glass, and a flash of lightning across the high ceiling. He reeled back in shock as a shower of sparks came swirling through the air towards him.

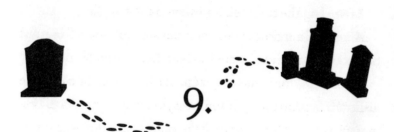

9.

A Word with the Electrical Wizard

Artie yelped and threw his arms up protectively in front of his face as sparks flickered all about him. When he lowered them, the electrical disturbance had ceased, leaving only a whiff of ozone in the air. Ham stepped cautiously into the hallway beside him, wide-eyed with alarm.

"Artie, what was that?" he asked.

Artie quickly pulled himself together and spoke confidently. "It's quite all right, Ham. It will just be one of the doctor's experiments. Come on in." They walked down the hallway, taking in the coils of blackened wire that dangled from the ceiling and shattered fragments of glass tubing that littered the carpet.

"Artie, are you sure you should be keeping company with someone as dangerous as this?" Ham asked, crunching a piece of glass beneath the sole of his boot.

"Oh, Dr Harthill's not dangerous," said Artie. "He's a real registered doctor. He just has lots of interesting and innovative ideas about medicine and science."

"Like this, for instance?" Ham paused to stare at a large diagram on the wall. "What on earth is this supposed to be?"

It was a drawing of a bald human head, the scalp criss-crossed with lines dividing it into labelled sections.

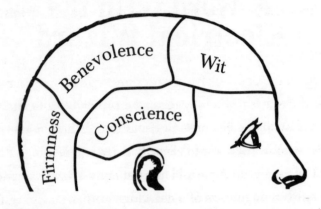

"Oh, that illustrates the principles of phrenology, the science of examining the skull," Artie explained. "From the shape of a man's head you can tell what sort of character he has, whether he's an intellectual, an artist or even a criminal."

"Are you saying a chap could be arrested just for the shape of his head?"

"I suppose that would be carrying it a bit too far. You'd still have to prove that he'd committed a crime."

"But if he had a criminal head, shouldn't you arrest him right away to keep him from committing a crime?"

"I think judges and lawyers would have a hard time wrestling with that," said Artie. "But I would like the opportunity to examine Benjamin Warren's head. I'm sure I would find some criminal bumps on his skull."

Artie led Ham down the long hallway, past framed scientific diagrams and photographs of grey-bearded, balding men posing at various medical conferences.

"And what was that sign on the door about Calvinism?" asked Ham.

"Not Calvinism, you dunce – galvanism. It's named after the Italian scientist Galvani who showed that you can make a dead frog's leg twitch by passing electricity through it."

Ham wrinkled his nose in distaste. "For goodness' sake, Artie, who would want to electrify a dead frog?"

"The theory is," Artie told him patiently, "that if electricity can enliven the nerves of a dead frog, perhaps it can restore health and vigour to sick people."

BZZZ-ZZZZZZ-CRRRREEAACKKK-FFFFF

"Listen, what's that noise?" Ham exclaimed.

A sporadic buzzing and crackling was coming from the door at the far end of the hallway.

"That's Doctor Harthill's laboratory," said Artie as they approached it. He knocked, but once again there was no reply. He opened the door – this time very cautiously.

A powerful tang of ozone suddenly stung their nostrils

and flashing zigzags of light forced them to shield their eyes.

Between the flashes of light, they glanced around to see shelves and tables supporting a dazzling array of scientific equipment.

There were large bottles of acid labelled with chemical formulae like H_2SO_4. Round plates of copper, iron and zinc had been stacked in columns and submerged in tanks of coloured liquid. Metal spheres crackled with sparks and all across the room trailed thick cables that buzzed continuously with electrical current.

In the middle of all this, in a large, wooden chair, sat Dr William Harthill, a wiry figure with a shock of silvered hair. He was in his shirtsleeves and fastened around his middle was a leather belt covered in a weave of metallic fibres. Coils of wire connected the belt to a series of batteries on a nearby table.

The doctor was so absorbed in feeling his own pulse and checking a row of dials that at first he didn't notice the visitors. The two boys stood in stunned silence amidst of the electrical chaos until he finally realised they were there.

"Ah, Mr Doyle!" Harthill exclaimed, his lean features lighting up in a welcoming smile. "How fortuitous that you should happen by!" He flicked a switch that protruded from the arm of his chair then unfastened the belt from around his waist. He stood up and stretched, then puffed out his chest like a man taking in a breath of fresh sea air.

"Dr Harthill," said Artie, "there's been some sort of explosion in the hallway."

"What, again?" The doctor tutted to himself. "I have been trying to light the hall using electricity but the filaments keep overheating and blowing out the tubes. Most unsatisfactory."

"I hope we're not interrupting," said Artie. "My friend Edward Hamilton and I wanted to ask you a few questions about galvanism."

"If it's a bad time we can just leave." Ham cast an eager glance at the door.

"Not at all, not at all." The doctor took an old tweed jacket from a nearby peg and slipped it on. "The two of you are the first to witness the workings of the new Harthill Galvanic Belt," he announced proudly. "The effects are truly remarkable."

"What does it do?" Ham inquired dubiously. "Give you the strength of ten men? Help you to live for a hundred years?"

"Nothing so frivolous, my young friend," Dr Harthill laughed. "No, no, no, this is a true breakthrough which will bring the most wondrous benefit to the human race. It is – at last – a complete and definitive cure for indigestion." He clapped his hands together and beamed with delight at his triumph.

"Am I understanding you right, Dr Harthill?" Artie gestured at the array of scientific equipment. "All of this is to cure indigestion?"

"Precisely!" the doctor enthused. He cast an eye over Ham and said, "You, my fine fellow, are surely familiar with the pain of indigestion that frequently follows a heavy meal."

"I wouldn't say that," Ham mumbled.

"In our modern times," Dr Harthill resumed, "when people consume unhealthy amounts of pies, dumplings and puddings, indigestion has become a blight upon society. But now that the power of electricity can provide relief, diners need not worry about the consequences of over-eating. Thanks to the Harthill Galvanic Belt, intestinal discomfort will be a thing of the past."

"I'm sure it's very useful," said Artie, "but you'd need a whole room for all the equipment."

Doctor Harthill scurried briskly about, flicking switches and pulling levers until the buzz and crackle of his electrical batteries subsided to a low hum.

"Oh, this is merely an experimental model, my boy. The final product will be quite portable. And," he added with a bright smile, "the sensation is so mild and soothing, even an infant could bear it."

"Artie, I don't know about you," said Ham in a confidential tone, "but I'd rather put up with a tummy ache than be wired up to all this gubbins."

Dr Harthill made a final adjustment to his equipment then turned back to face the boys. "So, Mr Doyle, has your father

78

shown any signs of improvement since you brought him to me for treatment?"

Artie's heart sank at the thought of his father's declining condition. "I can't say that he has, sir, much as I wish he would."

"Hmmm… unfortunate. Perhaps if I adjust the voltage."

"The world presses down on him, sir, and he hasn't the strength to bear the weight."

"Ah, well," said the doctor, "even the marvels of electrical science have not yet developed to the point of curing the spirit. But one day…" He raised a finger to demonstrate his confidence in the future.

"Actually, Dr Harthill," said Artie, "we're here to ask your advice about a recent spate of crimes that have the police baffled. We've been making some inquiries of our own."

"Good, good," Harthill enthused. "I believe an inquiring mind is the most important thing in the world." He perched himself on the edge of the chair. "So tell me all about it."

Artie gave him a brief account of the recent grave robberies, explaining how the stolen corpses had reappeared without any sign that they had been used for anatomical research.

"It is most curious," Harthill agreed. "And yet I don't see what insight I can offer."

"Well," Artie continued hesitantly, "I read a book in which it was suggested that electricity could be used to bring dead bodies back to life. Could our suspect have been attempting to do such a thing?"

Harthill let out a short, sharp laugh then stifled it by slapping a hand over his mouth.

"Forgive me," he said. "I don't mean to mock, but really…"

"But the frog, the twitching leg…"

"Mere reflex," said the doctor dismissively. "No, no. No amount of galvanic force can reanimate a body once the soul has flown. Only God could do that."

Artie's face turned red with embarrassment and frustration. "But you've proved how many ailments can be cured by electricity."

The doctor raised a hand to cut him off. "My boy, if you take a spoonful of tonic, it will give you renewed vigour. We can agree on that. But that doesn't mean that if you pour a bucket of tonic over a dead body it will miraculously spring to life and start dancing around the room, does it?"

"I suppose not," Artie conceded. "Then I have no idea why all those bodies were dug up. There must be a reason – and I can't shake off the feeling that Warren was involved."

"Sometimes, Artie, a mystery is just a mystery." Ham tried to console his friend. "There's no point beating your brains over it."

"I'm not interested in just saying it's a mystery and using that as an excuse to give up," said Artie stubbornly. He looked to Dr Harthill, who appeared to be lost in thought.

The doctor suddenly emerged from his reverie and jumped to his feet. "Your perseverance does you credit, my young friend."

"Do you have an idea then?" Artie inquired hopefully.

"Perhaps," said the doctor with an impish gleam in his eye, "you should be thinking about magic."

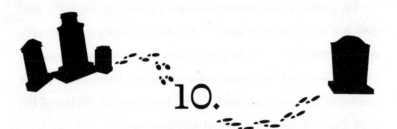

The Ghost Walks Again

"Magic?" Artie repeated incredulously. "Surely you don't believe in magic, doctor?"

"What? No, no," said Harthill, "not in spells and black cats and all that superstitious mumbo jumbo. No, I mean stage magic – which is of course trickery, but requires an impressive degree of skill and preparation."

Artie scratched his head in confusion. "I'm afraid I still don't follow you."

"I was once approached by the magician John Henry Anderson," said the doctor, "professionally known as the Wizard of the North."

"He's amazing!" Ham enthused. "We went to see him at the Palace Theatre and he made a lady float in the air and made a pony disappear and—"

"Yes, Ham," Artie cut him off. "We've all heard of him, but what did he want with you, Dr Harthill?"

"He wished to incorporate some of my electrical apparatus into his stage performance," the doctor replied, "to create spectacular effects. I told him I could not allow my research to be trivialised as mere entertainment. However, in the course of our discussions I learned one or two tricks of his craft. One of which is termed misdirection."

Ham wrinkled his nose in puzzlement. "Miswhatsit?"

"Misdirection: the art of distracting the audience with one hand," Doctor Harthill raised his right hand high above his head and wiggled his fingers, "whilst carrying out some unseen piece of trickery with the other." He brought out his left hand from behind his back, holding a pencil he had plucked from Ham's pocket.

"But what has that got to do with the grave robberies, sir?"

"Consider this possibility, my friend," said the doctor. "Could it be that the discarded bodies are a distraction, causing the police and yourselves to investigate body-snatching for medical research? During which time you are not asking yourselves: What are these mysterious characters really digging up? Could there be something else hidden in those graves?"

This was the question Artie took away with him when they left the doctor's office. As he and Ham walked along Rutland

Street, he kept his hands thrust deep into his pockets and stared intently at the pavement, as though trying to reach an answer that lay hidden in the earth.

"You know, Artie, it's getting dark." Ham cast a glance up at the winter sky. "We really should go home and see what's for tea."

Artie's only response was a distracted grunt.

"I don't know about you," his friend went on, "but I always do my best thinking on a full stomach. After all, how can your brain concentrate if your stomach keeps rumbling. I'll bet all the great thinkers like Socrates and St Augustine did their best cogitating somewhere between the steak and kidney pie and the plum pudding."

Artie roused abruptly from his reverie, as if only now becoming aware of his surroundings.

"Dr Harthill is a very clever man," he said. "I'm quite sure he's on to something."

"You're right," Ham agreed. "We should hand the whole case over to him and let him solve it. After all, we'll be heading back to Stonyhurst in a couple of days. Best clear the mind and get ready for all that Latin and algebra."

"We're not going anywhere until we find the answer to this mystery," Artie declared firmly. "What we need to do, Ham, is visit the scenes of the crimes."

"What? Now?" Ham objected. "Visit three separate graveyards? That will take all night!"

"If Dr Harthill is right, and the bodies are just a blind

for what's really going on, we may find clues at the graves themselves."

"On second thoughts," Ham replied, "I'm not convinced old Harthill's so smart after all. Most likely putting all those volts through his innards has unbalanced his mind."

Artie ignored him and continued to ponder the problem.

They turned into Lothian Road, which was much busier than the peaceful elegance of Rutland Square. Horse-drawn vehicles rumbled by and many people were bustling along the pavement, wrapped up in overcoats and scarves. Artie pressed his hand over his nose as they passed a man shovelling horse manure off the street into a cart. Ham coughed and rubbed his eyes, which were watering from the stink.

Suddenly Artie seized his friend by the arm and yanked him into a narrow close.

"Look!" He directed Ham's attention to the other side of the street. "It's Warren!"

"What, your lodger? The criminal mastermind himself?" Ham peered across at the pale young man in the dark coat. "And who's that with him? Oh, Artie, it looks like…" His voice tailed off in horror.

"Yes," said Artie, "it looks like the Lady in Grey."

The girl at Warren's side looked about nineteen years old and she was wrapped in the same long cloak they had seen at Greyfriars Kirkyard. The hood had fallen back onto her shoulders to reveal a pretty, delicate face and light brown hair tied behind in a black ribbon. She was sobbing and dabbing at her tears with a small white kerchief.

"She certainly looks like she's grieving for her lost sweetheart," said Ham wonderingly, "just like in the story."

"Well, she's not likely to find him buried in the middle of Lothian Road," said Artie, "so I think we can forget about the legend."

Warren and the girl stopped in front of a milliner's shop and he tried to comfort her without drawing too much attention from passers-by.

"If she's not a ghost," said Ham, "then what was she doing at Greyfriars in the middle of the night? She certainly doesn't look strong enough to go around digging up graves."

"No, but Warren could. He's probably tricked her into thinking he's a jolly fine fellow and all that in order to misuse her somehow."

"So what are we going to do?" asked Ham.

"We should go over there and confront him," Artie said boldly. "Expose him for the villain he is, right in front of the girl."

"Let's not cause a scene, Artie," Ham cautioned. "After all, you've no evidence that he's actually done anything villainous."

Artie shuffled his feet and chewed his lip, desperate to take some course of action. Before he could come to a decision a voice rang out from further up the road.

"Warren! Ho, Warren! Is that you there?"

At the sound of that voice, Warren immediately pressed the girl into the shop doorway, out of sight. He then turned and strolled briskly up the road, as though he were completely alone.

Striding towards him was a tall, rakish figure in a long frock coat. His long chestnut hair was elegantly styled and his moustache and sideburns had been neatly clipped to give him an aristocratic appearance. He carried a gold-handled cane with which he struck the ground as he walked, as if he was beating the earth itself into submission.

When the two men met, they struck up what appeared to be a tense conversation: Warren took on the demeanour of a humble servant while the other man questioned him intently. Artie wished he could hear what they were saying, but they were too far away. A horse-drawn bus rumbled by with an advertisement for Dairymaid Condensed Milk plastered down its side, briefly blocking his view.

"I really think we should go home," Ham urged nervously for the umpteenth time that day. "That chap over there doesn't look like the sort of man you want to get mixed up with. Not if you value your well-being."

Artie knew what his friend meant. There was an air of confident menace about the newcomer that clearly had the young medical student cowed. The two men turned and walked off together up Lothian Road.

"I'm going to follow those two, Ham."

"Follow them?" Ham bleated. "You don't expect me to come along, do you?"

"No, no, that would make us too conspicuous. Wait here and follow that girl to wherever she goes."

"But, Artie," Ham's voice dropped to an anxious whisper, "suppose she really is a ghost? Who knows where she might lead me?"

"If she leads you to her grave, take a note of the name on the stone," Artie instructed, "then report to me in the morning."

"I say, you're not being serious, are you?" Ham pleaded.

For an answer, Artie darted across the road in pursuit of Warren and the other man, leaving Ham to decide for himself.

Artie soon discovered how tricky it was to shadow the pair. He had to keep a safe distance so they wouldn't spot him, without losing sight of them among the busy crowds. A short way up Lothian Road, the tall man hailed a horse-drawn cab, which pulled up beside them. He and Warren climbed aboard and the tall man gave instructions to the driver that Artie couldn't hear.

As the cab pulled off, Artie hurried after it. There was only one way to find out what they were up to. He had once seen a pair of street urchins jump onto the luggage shelf projecting from the back of a cab, taking a free ride just for a lark. When the cabbie noticed them, he stopped and chased after them with his horsewhip.

Artie's purpose was more serious and he was prepared to risk getting into trouble. He caught up with the cab as it gathered speed and scrambled onto the shelf, seizing hold of the leather straps intended to hold baggage in place.

Through a small window in the back of the cab he could see the heads of the two men engaged in conversation. He curled up below their line of sight in case either of them should take a backward glance.

He strained his ears over the rumble of the wheels and the clip-clop of the horse's hooves to hear what they were saying. One voice, at any rate, made itself clearly heard.

"When you receive a summons from *me*, Colonel Braxton Dash, I expect you to come running," the tall man in the frock coat was saying. "I should not have to keep looking for you."

Artie's heart skipped a beat when he heard this.

Keep looking! Those were the exact words and the same tone of commanding arrogance he had heard at Greyfriars Kirkyard that night. This was the very man who had been there giving orders.

Warren made some unhappy comment and Colonel Braxton Dash laughed.

"Cheer up, Warren!" he urged contemptuously. "You're in for a jolly evening with the Gravediggers' Club."

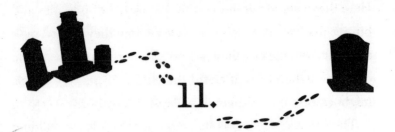

11.

The Master of the Black Hound

Artie caught very little of whatever else passed between Warren and Colonel Braxton Dash. The cab rattled and bumped from side to side and it was all he could do to stay on his precarious perch and avoid being hurled to the ground. As he clung desperately to the luggage straps, the last words of the tall man echoed in his mind like the ringing of an alarm.

The Gravediggers' Club.

If the stranger was a member of that club, he was surely its leader, for he had the air of a man who wouldn't take orders from anyone else. And he suspected they had nothing to do with the honourable work of digging graves, like John Dalhousie.

They soon left the great buildings of the city behind, passing through Morningside and beyond the Braid Hills.

Here they veered left into a rutted track full of potholes and bumps that jarred Artie's spine every time they passed over one. Far from the city they passed a scattering of ramshackle cottages. Artie was half afraid the clatter of the cab wheels might cause some of them to collapse into rubble.

The sun was sinking as they approached a large building of faded red brick and rotted timber. As the cab slowed down, Artie slid from his perch and scurried into the cover of some bushes. The cabman reined in his horse and the passengers climbed out.

The long-neglected building had boarded-up windows and tiles missing from the roof. Above the doorway hung a lopsided sign with flaking paint:

Arbuthnott and Cole
Leatherworkers

It had clearly been many years since any leather had been worked here. Nevertheless a dozen assorted wagons and carriages were parked round about. Clearly some business was afoot.

Once they had paid the cabbie, Warren and his companion headed for the entrance. A burly, bearded individual greeted them gruffly as he opened the door. Shutting the door behind them, he began cleaning his fingernails with a small knife while keeping one eye peeled for more arrivals.

Not knowing what was going on inside, Artie couldn't think of any way to bluff his way past this imposing guard. He crept around to the rear of the building, keeping to the shadows of bushes and trees, looking for a back entrance. Several large wooden vats lay discarded there which, he assumed from the smell, had once been used for soaking leather. Crouching behind one of these, he surveyed his surroundings.

Off to his right was a midden: a pile of unsavoury rubbish that had accumulated over the years. Beyond the midden lay a shallow ditch from which wafted the stench of stagnant water and decaying refuse. In the rear wall of the building he observed four boarded-up windows and a small door that was firmly closed.

Now that he was here, alone in the cold and deepening dark, he began to regret the impulse that had sent him rushing off on this dangerous quest. It would take him a couple of hours to walk home from here, even if he could find his way.

Unless he discovered more about the Gravediggers' Club and uncovered some criminal activity, this whole rash adventure would be a waste of time. Perhaps McCorkle had been right in his dull, practical way. Perhaps reading adventure stories wasn't proper preparation for this sort of detective work.

Just then the door creaked open and a skinny, bald-headed man in an apron came out, carrying a bucket. He stumped around the midden with his back to Artie's hiding place.

The yellow light streaming from the open doorway fired Artie's resolve and he started forward in a low crouch. If he could just get inside while the man was occupied…

The bald man tipped the foul-smelling contents of the bucket into the ditch, then turned just in time to catch sight of Artie making for the door.

"Hey! What are you after?"

Artie froze in mid-step and gaped in horror as the man in the apron came striding towards him. He tried to think of some story to explain his presence here, but the man's hostile gaze seemed to rob him of the power of speech. He stood there as mute as a haddock while the bald man advanced on him with a scowl.

"Here, are you the boy they've sent in place of Weezil?" he demanded.

"Weezil?" Artie echoed. It dawned on him that there was an opportunity here and he decided to seize it. "Er, yes, that's right, in his place… What's happened to Weezil exactly?"

The man's scowl deepened. "Dose of the croup, wasn't it? Surely they told you."

"Oh, yes, of course, dose of the croup it was." Artie tried to sound confident and not at all like a nervous imposter. "Mr Weezil asked me personally to offer his apologies," he added, hoping this would banish any suspicions.

"I don't care a maggot's spit for his apologies," snorted the bald man. "You get yourself inside and set to work."

"Yes, yes, right away." Artie obediently hurried to the door. He realised he had to grab his chance before Weezil's actual replacement showed up, or in case Weezil himself made a sudden recovery.

"And take this privy bucket with you!" barked the man.

Artie backtracked a few steps, caught the outstretched bucket by the handle, and plunged into the disused leatherworks.

Inside it was as busy as a market and just as noisy. The walls of the large room were made of plain, discoloured brick, and the whole place was lit by oil lanterns which gave off a greasy smell. A score of rickety tables had been set up where groups of men played games of chance with dice and cards, greeting each turn of fortune with a roar of triumph or a groan of despair.

Artie set down the bucket and moved through the crowd with his head down, doing his best not to draw attention to himself. In the far left corner of the room a fiddler played a lively jig, to which some couples were dancing unsteadily.

Off to the right a dozen chairs had been set up on a raised stage. Here sat Colonel Braxton Dash, gazing down at the gathering like a king surveying his court. Seated around him was a band of men that Artie guessed were his fellow 'gravediggers'. Their round tables were laden with platters of roast chicken, cheese and bread, along with bottles of wine and tankards of ale. A pair of women in grubby aprons and thick make-up passed among the company, replenishing their drinks.

What really caught Artie's eye, however, was the huge black dog lying on the floor at Dash's left hand. It was a ferocious-looking mastiff wearing a studded leather collar. Its long leash was wrapped around the arm of the colonel's chair. Artie had no doubt that this was the beast whose eerie howls had so unnerved him at Greyfriars Kirk.

At Dash's other hand sat Benjamin Warren, his head bowed low, toying unhappily with an empty glass. He looked uncomfortable in this raucous company and for an instant Artie felt a twinge of sympathy for the young student. Then he recalled that Warren had brought the police to their door, and finding him in this disreputable place only confirmed his suspicions that the lodger was up to no good.

Dash stood up and twirled his gold-handled cane

95

flamboyantly in one hand before rapping it three times on the stage. At this signal the hubbub died down to a scattering of murmurs and whispers.

"Fellow Gravediggers, friends and honoured guests," Dash addressed the crowd in a loud, commanding voice. "I also include, of course, toadies, hangers on, and," he added with a thin smile, "those who have sneaked in to rob the place."

Sneaked in! Artie's blood ran cold with sheer terror. Dash must mean him. He had been spotted. And now here he was defenceless in the hands of a band of ruthless cutthroats!

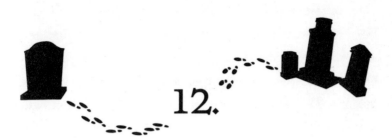

The Meeting of the Fighting Men

Artie stood paralysed with fear amidst the crowd of revellers. But instead of taking him prisoner, the whole place burst into peals of coarse laughter. He realised, to his relief and joy, that nobody was even looking at him. Braxton Dash was just making a crude joke.

"As you all know," the colonel went on, "we Gravediggers like nothing better than rich food, strong drink, and winning!"

This prompted another outburst of coarse laughter as members of the crowd rattled their money bags.

"But one more thing we enjoy is an expert demonstration of the manly art of fisticuffs."

As he spoke, the centre of the room was being cleared. Men appeared with ropes and wooden stanchions and started cordoning off a large square. Artie realised at once what they were doing: they were setting up a boxing ring.

Dash resumed his seat as two fighters entered the ring. A buzz of excitement washed over the crowd. The contestants were stripped to the waist, showing off their muscled chests. One was a towering giant of a man with heavy, stolid features. The other was shorter, but wiry and athletic. Artie judged they were both fit enough to provide a first-class contest. All around the room bundles of notes appeared and coins jingled as bets were made on the outcome of the fight.

The referee, who, judging by his broken nose, appeared to be a former boxer himself, moved to the centre of the ring and waved his arms to quiet the crowd. He gestured first at the big man and announced loudly, "Presenting for your sporting appreciation, on my right, the man-mountain, the battling behemoth of Musselburgh, Bruno 'The Slogger' Buchanan!"

Cheers and applause greeted The Slogger, but the man mountain's heavy face showed no flicker of emotion.

The referee turned to the shorter contestant, who was shuffling his feet and jabbing energetically at the empty air.

"And on my left," he continued, "the twinkle-toed terror of Portobello, the man his own shadow can't catch, 'Dancing' Donny Drew!"

Donny skipped around the ring, acknowledging the cheers of the crowd, before he and his opponent took up position on either side of the referee.

Artie noticed that they were going to box bare-knuckled,

a style which remained popular with those who wanted their sport to be as rough as possible. The referee was giving the two men their instructions: no kicking, no gouging, no wrestling and, above all, no hitting a man when he was down – the contest certainly seemed honourable. As the long list of rules came to an end, the Slogger's expression did not change, but Artie saw him cast a glance up at the colonel, who gave him a slight nod and a sly wink.

Unaware of what had passed between the two men, Dancing Donny was bouncing on the spot and jabbing his fists first in one direction then the other, as if warding off a pair of invisible opponents. Artie had the uneasy sense that something was amiss with this contest.

The fighters backed into opposite corners, where each man had two attendants to wash him down between rounds and patch up his injuries. After receiving some words of advice from their corners, both men came up to the middle of the ring.

It was then that the referee signalled the start of the contest and the whole crowd cheered. The fighters moved to the attack, the Slogger lumbering forward like an ox, while Dancing Donny pranced this way and that, his head bobbing from side to side.

With everyone's attention on the fight, Artie took the chance to slip unnoticed through the crowd, working his way towards the stage where Warren and Dash were seated.

He passed a group of red-faced men whose beery breath almost choked him.

Glancing back at the ring, he saw that the pattern of the match was becoming clear: Dancing Donny moved in nimble circles around his opponent, poking him in the face and midriff with precise jabs. The Slogger took the punishment without any sign of discomfort, choosing his moment to lurch onto the attack with a swinging blow that either missed or glanced off the other man's shoulder.

The crowd became more and more excited, yelling and cheering and changing their bets as the rounds progressed. Artie ducked beneath their waving arms and wove around their stamping feet. Keeping his head down low, he sneaked up a small set of stairs onto the stage and sidled up beside a group of men behind Warren and Dash. He was careful to keep well clear of the great hound that lay at its master's side.

"I don't know why you have to take that beast everywhere with you," he heard Warren remark with an unhappy glance at the dog. "He's hardly inconspicuous."

"Erebus is the only one of my partners I trust," said the colonel, scratching the animal behind the ears. "If anyone tries to interfere in my business, Erebus has a way of dissuading them." He gave a cold smile. "He has other uses too, as you will see."

Their next few words were drowned out as the crowd roared its approval of a pair of well-placed jabs from Dancing

Donny. Betting around the room was moving in Donny's favour with every round that passed.

When the noise subsided, Artie could hear Warren speaking again.

"You know how he felt about the six hundred. And she feels the same way."

"Devil take the six hundred, man!" cursed Braxton Dash. "I'll find better use for it than that."

"I don't like it," Warren grumbled. "This affair is far too risky."

"You don't have to like it," Dash responded with a sneer. "Either you'll work off your debt this way, or I'll invent a method you'll find considerably more painful."

Warren hung his head low. "As you say," he conceded.

The colonel drummed his fingers on the arm of his chair. "Tomorrow we'll try our luck at Calton."

The two men exchanged a few more remarks, which Artie couldn't make out over the roar of the crowd. How he wished he could hear exactly what they were talking about. Who was this Braxton Dash, and what on earth was the Six Hundred?

At least he knew where they were heading tomorrow – Calton, another cemetery on Warren's list. Artie smiled inwardly. He had been right to persist with his investigations. He was fired with a new determination to solve this case and prove both Ham and Constable McCorkle wrong.

Colonel Braxton Dash now focused his full attention on the boxers. Halfway through the seventh round, Artie saw him surreptitiously curl a hand around the dog's leash and give it two sharp tugs. The giant hound promptly jumped up on its massive paws and set up a terrible barking. Everyone on the stage recoiled in horror from the blood-curdling noise and it was all Artie could do not to dive for cover under a chair.

Dancing Donny's footwork died on the spot and he instinctively spun round towards the source of the din. The Slogger, on the other hand, seemed completely unaware of the beast's awful barking. While his opponent was distracted, he drew back an enormous fist and sent it crashing into the side of the smaller man's head. Dancing Donny dropped to the floor as if the very life had been knocked out of him.

Artie glanced back at Colonel Dash and saw him give the leash another tug. The hound immediately fell silent and sank back down on the floor.

Donny lay motionless. His supporters let out a groan of despair and those who had laid money on the Slogger whooped in triumph.

The referee knelt down beside the fallen fighter. "Are ye alright, lad?"

Donny groaned weakly and made a feeble effort to rise before sinking back down on the floor.

"Aye, ye'll be fine," the referee assured him. "Somebody

fetch him a dram!" He stood up and took hold of the Slogger by one hand. Raising the big man's brawny arm into the air, he declared, "I give you your winner, Bruno 'The Slogger' Buchanan!"

There were renewed cheers for the victor, though he himself appeared completely unmoved by all the fuss. A well-dressed, weak-chinned young man standing close to Artie leaned forward and clapped the colonel on the shoulder.

"Bless me, Dash," he laughed, "you're the very devil for picking a winner!"

Warren turned irritably at the sound of the braying laugh and his eyes flared as he caught sight of Artie.

Artie realised he was in serious danger if the young student decided to expose him as a spy. He began to back away, but before he could take more than a step, he was seized by the arm and yanked forward.

He was caught in the unyielding grip of Colonel Braxton Dash.

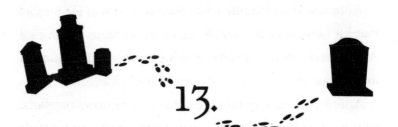

Concerning Colonel
Braxton Dash

Impulsively Artie tried to wrench himself free, but as soon as he did, the black hound swung its large, jowly face in his direction. A low, threatening growl rumbled in its throat. Artie immediately abandoned his struggle, his eyes fixed anxiously on the ferocious animal.

"Don't fret yourself, boy." Colonel Braxton Dash gave a dry chuckle. "He'll not eat you. Not unless I tell him to."

There was a murmur of unpleasant laughter as the colonel's friends shared his mirth.

Warren was staring at Artie, his face a mask of confusion and indecision. "Dash…" he began hesitantly.

Paying the medical student no mind, the colonel said to Artie, "Now listen, boy. I've a raging thirst on me. Go to the back room and fetch me a bottle of gin. I'll drink it while I count my winnings."

Artie saw Warren settle back in his seat with evident relief that his landlady's son was to come to no harm. Dash sent Artie on his way with a shove and his companions continued to congratulate him on the victory of his fighter.

Artie wove his way through the crowd of noisy revellers, who were either celebrating with toasts or drowning their sorrows. Their games of cards and dice resumed while they chattered about the boxing match, some giving their imitation of The Slogger's victorious blow.

The room beyond was a combined kitchen and pantry housing barrels of beer, crates of wine and many bottles of spirits, as well as various foodstuffs. A hatchet-faced woman with frizzled grey hair was snapping orders at a few harassed-looking servants.

"What do you want?" she challenged Artie in a voice as harsh as a raven's. "I don't know you, you wee tyke."

Artie could see a door at the far side of the room, but he would have to get past the woman to reach it.

"I've come for gin," he asserted, deciding that playing it bold was his best chance. "I've been sent for it and I mean to have some."

"Gin? For who?" the woman asked sharply.

"For the colonel," Artie answered quickly. The last thing he wanted to do was rejoin Colonel Braxton Dash and risk being exposed by Benjamin Warren, but for now he had to tough things out with Hatchet Face.

105

"You're ower smartly dressed to be working here," the woman rasped suspiciously, "and you're too much of a bairn to be one of the colonel's guests. So who are you?"

"I'm… I'm…" Artie stammered. He tried to think of some answer that would take the hostile gleam out of her eye, but could think of nothing that sounded plausible.

"I'll answer for the boy," came a voice. It was Warren, marching hurriedly into the room. "And Colonel Dash is wanting his gin." He grabbed a bottle of the liquor from a nearby shelf and thrust it not at Artie but at a passing servant. "Here, get this to the colonel as quick as you can, before his mood turns sour."

The servant hurried off with the bottle in a tight embrace. The hard-faced woman's attention was suddenly caught by another servant who was clumsily preparing a platter of food.

"What? Are you cutting the ham with a cleaver?" she screeched. "Use a knife, curse you!"

She seized the incompetent underling by the hair and gave him a good shake.

Warren took advantage of the distraction to shove Artie to the door and propel him outside.

"You can't stay here," he said in a tense undertone. "This place is dangerous enough for me, let alone for a boy of your tender years."

"There's nothing tender about me," Artie told him bullishly.

"Well, I'm getting us out of here anyway," Warren insisted, leading Artie by the arm to where the cabs and wagons were parked. He bundled Artie into a cab and climbed into the seat beside him. "Take us back into town," he instructed the driver. "I'll give you the address later."

The driver started his horse with a flick of the reins and the cab lurched into motion.

Warren stared hard at Artie, as if the intensity of his gaze might force an explanation. "How did you find this place?"

Artie folded his arms doggedly. "I have my methods."

Warren shook his head in exasperation. "You have no idea what you've walked into." He kept his voice low so the driver wouldn't hear over the horse's hoofbeats.

"I have a few ideas," Artie retorted. "I must say that friend of yours doesn't look like he digs graves for a living."

"Braxton Dash is no one's friend," said Warren unhappily. "And he doesn't practise any honest trade, let alone working in a graveyard."

"But he and his cronies call themselves the Gravediggers' Club, don't they?" Artie challenged, meeting Warren's eyes squarely.

The student winced at the mention of the club then gave a half-hearted smile.

"It's a joke," he explained. "Colonel Dash and his friends lead lives of such reckless excess and dangerous thrill seeking, they say that they're digging their own graves."

"A colonel, eh?" said Artie. "He doesn't strike me as a military man."

"Oh, he's no officer, you can be sure of that," said Warren sourly. "He just calls himself 'colonel' and everybody else falls into line. I'd wager his name isn't really Braxton Dash either."

"So in fact he's nothing but a fraud."

"Whatever he is, he lords it over everyone as if he were Napoleon himself."

"Has he then," said Artie, pressing his point carefully, "never had anything to do with any graves?" He watched Warren closely for his reaction.

The student was definitely discomfited by the question and looked away quickly. "Arthur, whatever it is you think you know, forget about it," he advised sternly. "There's nothing for you in this matter but mortal danger."

"I can see that he gambles, and not honestly either," said Artie. "Is that how you're mixed up with him? Because you owe him money?"

Warren's whole frame stiffened and a muscle pulsed in his jaw. "I'm taking you home now, Artie. I'll have the cabbie drop us some distance from there, so if he's ever questioned, there will be no direct connection between your household and that dreadful place where we met tonight."

"I suppose that's wise," Artie conceded. He certainly didn't want his parents ever to learn that he'd been in a house of such dubious repute. They would probably drag him along to confession to tell all to Father Ramsay.

"And let me make this point most emphatically," Warren added. "You and I will never speak of these matters again."

Artie said nothing, but in his own mind he promised himself that he would not let these matters rest until he had discovered what it was that bound together the lodger, the Gravediggers' Club and the six stolen corpses.

The Riddle of the
Six Hundred

"Well, I'm deuced if I can see any connection!" Ham exclaimed. "It seems to me that the deeper we delve into this mystery the more obscure it becomes."

It was the middle of the following afternoon and the two boys had taken refuge from the rain inside the newly opened Edinburgh Museum of Science and Art in Chambers Street. Not only were their clothes damp from the winter shower, their boots were caked in mud from trudging around graveyards most of the day. They had visited each of the six robbed graves that morning, looking for any clues to connect them with Warren, the Gravediggers' Club or the Lady in Grey.

"Calm yourself, Ham," said Artie as they sat down on a bench in a large gallery with high ceilings. "We just need time to think and review the facts."

Ham gazed half-heartedly at the exhibits. There was a miniature steam engine, the skeleton of an extinct lizard, and portraits of several prominent engineers and chemists. From an adjacent gallery came the voice of a guide explaining to a group of school children the burial customs of the ancient Egyptians.

Artie flipped through the pages of his journal, where he had recorded all the information he had gathered so far.

Sunday, January 21, 1872

Trailed Warren to disused leatherworks outside of town. He was in the company of Col. Braxton Dash, chief of the so-called Gravediggers' Club.

What is the 600?

What do they hope to find at Calton?

Monday, January 22, 1872

Visited all 6 graves on McCorkle's list and took notes from gravestones. What is the connection?

"Ham," he said, "tell me again what happened when you followed the Lady in Grey."

Ham immediately perked up. He clearly relished the fact that he had his own important role in the investigation.

"Well, she left the doorway of the milliner's shortly after you raced off after your lodger. I played it canny, hanging back so she wouldn't suspect I was on her trail. I was paying such attention to her that I bumped into three or four people along the way. One of them called me a name I didn't care for, but he was a big chap, so I didn't make an issue of it."

"Yes, I remember you told me that," said Artie. "Get on with it."

"So off we went up the road," Ham resumed. "She stopped briefly outside a pharmacist's and the sight of it seemed to upset her afresh, you know, as if it brought back bad memories."

"Yes, that is interesting," Artie mused.

"Then she crossed the road and I had to move pretty smartly to keep up. I nearly got run over by a coal wagon. Honestly, those coal men really don't look where they're going and they use some highly uncouth language."

"I can see you faced some terrible dangers."

"Absolutely right," Ham affirmed. "Anyway, undaunted, I kept the Lady in Grey in my sights all the way up Lothian Road and into Bread Street. I did lose track of her briefly when I was passing a bakery. They were advertising Dundee cake and iced buns in the window."

"That's not really relevant," Artie sighed, as a group of visitors bustled past in search of a stuffed polar bear.

"If you didn't want a full report you should have said so," Ham huffed. "I did catch up in time to see her turn into Bread Street Lane. But when I got to the lane myself, she had disappeared." He waved his hands about mysteriously. "Vanished into thin air."

"Or more likely she entered one of the houses there."

"Well, yes," Ham admitted. "I was just trying to make the story interesting."

"Couldn't you have knocked on a few doors and tried to find her?"

"Knocked on doors? And said what? Excuse me, you don't happen to have a ghost hiding in here, do you? A fine thing that would be! They'd have locked me up as a lunatic."

"Well," said Artie, "at least we've established a connection between Warren and the girl we saw at Greyfriars Kirkyard, as well as between him and this professional rogue who calls himself Colonel Braxton Dash. It was definitely his voice we heard in the graveyard that night."

"And his dog we heard too, from what you've told me."

"Yes, and I still feel certain that those dratted six graves bind them all together. But how? Let's look at what we've learned about them." He glanced shiftily around at the other visitors to check none were eavesdropping then displayed the list for Ham's inspection. "See here, on this left-hand page, I've written down the names as they were given to us by Constable McCorkle. Now here on the facing page are the names as they are actually recorded on the gravestones."

Donald Cafferty	Donald Cafferty
Charles Tennant	Dr Charles Tennant
William Bruce	William Bruce DCM
Richard Chisholm	Richard 'Dickie' Chisholm
Daisy O'Connor	Daisy O'Connor
Marie de Certeau	Marie de Certeau

"Yes, there are a few small differences," said Ham. "But still…"

Artie whipped out his pencil and began tapping the page with it.

"Don't tell me you've cracked it!" said Ham.

"Not exactly," said Artie with an excited gleam in his eye. "I was studying the list during your… er… most interesting narrative, and I've finally spotted a pattern." He rapidly underscored certain letters on the right-hand page. "Now look at this!"

_Donald _Cafferty_

_Dr _Charles Tennant_

William Bruce _DCM_

Richard '_Dickie' _Chisholm_

_Daisy O'_Connor_

Marie _de _Certeau_

"D and C?" said Ham doubtfully. "Well, yes, I'm sure thousands of perfectly ordinary names have the letters D and C in them. Yours does: Arthur Conan Doyle."

"Yes, of course," said Artie, "but very few names would have them as initial letters in the right order, D then C, or beside each other, as in the case of William Bruce DCM."

"What's DCM?" Ham asked.

"It stands for Distinguished Conduct Medal. It's a medal given to soldiers for gallantry in the field."

"It could still just be a coincidence," said Ham dubiously. "I can't see that a couple of letters mean anything."

Artie chewed the end of his pencil so hard flakes of wood came off in his mouth. Suddenly he jumped up, waving the notebook in triumph.

"No, it's not a coincidence, and I have the proof of that!"

"Artie, sit down. You're creating a scene."

A museum attendant was looking at them sternly and shaking his head.

"Now what on earth are you talking about?" said Ham.

Artie sat back down and gave his friend a poke with the pencil. "Remember your Roman numerals!" he urged him excitedly. "You know, from Latin class."

"Roman numerals? Why should I want to remember them? Frankly they always made my head hurt."

"Because the letter D was used by the Romans to represent the number five hundred," Artie explained. "And the letter C represented one hundred."

Ham stared at him blankly.

"Don't you see? Put them together and you make the number six hundred. It must point to the same six hundred

Warren and Dash were talking about in that terrible place last night."

"Six hundred what?" Ham exclaimed "Miles? Graves? Bottles?"

Artie twirled the pencil over and over in his fingers. "I don't know that yet," he admitted. "But I'm going to find out."

"Really? And how are you going to do that?"

Artie's jaw tightened. "Dash said he was going to try his luck at Calton tonight."

"What, at Calton Hill?"

"He must have been talking about Calton Burial Ground."

"So what about it?" Ham's face was so dismal, he obviously wasn't looking forward to the answer.

"We're going to get there ahead of him, Ham," Artie declared. "We'll catch him in the act and get to the bottom of this affair at last!"

15.

Into the Valley of Death

An icy breeze whispered down Nicolson Street as two figures, hugging themselves against the cold, trudged across town. The pavements were slick with the day's rain and, as the midnight hour approached, the gas lamps formed yellow haloes in the drifting mist.

Ham shivered and pressed a hand to his mouth to keep his teeth from chattering.

"I can't believe I'm following you into another graveyard," he said wearily. "And in the middle of the night again. It's a good thing my mother is a sound sleeper. And that she snores, so I can hear when she's dozed off."

"With any luck this will be the last time we go searching in a graveyard." Artie tried to sound reassuring.

"Luck?" said Ham. "The only luck we've had so far is not being murdered by crooks or eaten by ghouls. I don't know why… why…" He stopped suddenly and remained standing where he was until Artie realised he wasn't following.

Puzzled, Artie turned back and rejoined his friend. "What's the matter, Ham? Don't you feel well?"

"That's just it, Artie," Ham groaned. "I am sick of this business. Why do you keep dragging me along? Why don't you get somebody more adventurous to accompany you? Or even a faithful dog?"

Artie was struck dumb. He rubbed his arms for a few seconds then cleared his throat. "Because I need you by my side, Ham. You know, as my stalwart companion."

"Is that because the heroes in your books always have a stalwart companion?" Ham retorted. "One who isn't quite as clever or brave as they are?"

There was a hurt in his voice that Artie had never heard before and it made him feel queasy inside. "N-no, it's not like that at all, Ham," he stammered.

"Is it just to keep me from the cakes then?" Ham pressed. "That's what you said when we started all these capers."

Both of them stared in silence at the rain-soaked pavement, casting only the occasional glance towards each other.

"I had to say something to persuade you," Artie muttered at last. Somehow the night seemed even colder than before.

"Really?" Ham's hands were thrust deep into his pockets, and under his cap his face had withdrawn into the upturned collar of his coat.

"The truth is…" Artie stamped his feet a few times to get the feeling back into his toes. "The truth is… I need you."

"Need me for what?" Ham wiped a sleeve across his damp nose. "I don't know anything about medical Calvinism—"

"Galvanism."

"Or how to trick cannibals. I couldn't even follow that ghost girl without losing her."

"None of that matters. The point is…" Artie paused as, off in the distance, somewhere on the Forth, a tugboat sounded its mournful horn. "The point is, you give me courage."

"Me? Give you courage?" Ham's voice was husky with incredulity.

"Yes," Artie said, "it is a dangerous venture and, to tell you the truth, I don't have the nerve for it all by myself."

Ham considered this for a moment. "I am pretty scared, you know. I don't mind admitting it."

"We both are. But when you lost your father," said Artie with a catch in his voice, "getting through that, taking care of your mother, that calls for a special kind of bravery. I can only hope that I would be half as brave."

Ham looked abashed. He gave a very forced shrug. "A chap does what he must."

"Yes, he does." Artie's frozen lips formed a smile.

"And sometimes, I suppose, he must be a stalwart companion." Slowly Ham's round face emerged from the shadow of his upturned collar into the pale gaslight. He was smiling too.

Artie clapped him heartily on the back. "Come on then, old fellow! We have work to do!"

They set off again, and suddenly, as though the winter night had eased its grip, they both felt warmer.

"My mother takes good care of me too, you know," said Ham. "Many's the time she's said to me, 'We may not have much, Eddie, but I'll not have anyone say you look ill fed.'"

"She's succeeded admirably," Artie assured him.

They crossed North Bridge and turned into Waterloo Place, then halted before the entrance to Calton Burial Ground. Beyond the graveyard, the dark mass of Calton prison was a sombre reminder of the danger they might be walking into. As at Greyfriars, the lock had been tampered with and the gate opened easily.

"You don't suppose they're here already, do you?" Ham wondered as they entered, carefully closing the gate behind them.

Artie signalled him to silence and led the way up the sloping path between the graves. He picked out a large tombstone on the left and they crouched down behind it. Through floating shrouds of mist they glimpsed a tall granite obelisk at the top of the rise, pointing up at the sky like a warning finger.

"No sign of anybody that I can see," Artie muttered.

"We'll be lucky to spot them in this murk."

"Keep a watch on the path. Colonel Dash will be here,"

Artie said confidently, "to dig up a grave marked with those letters D and C. I expect he's had one of his men scout it out in daylight."

"I'm not sure we'll learn much by watching out for him."

"If we keep our ears sharp," said Artie, "we may overhear them say what it is they're looking for."

"Something to do with the mysterious six hundred."

Artie nodded and gave an affirmative grunt.

Ham shifted his position to ease a cramp in his leg. "You know, Artie, there's something familiar about that number and it's been nagging at me."

"Yes, it's probably got something to do with mathematics." Artie rubbed his knees.

"No, not sums, Artie. Poetry."

"Poetry? Ham, it's not like you to talk about poetry." He stared at his friend and saw that his face was screwed up in intense concentration.

"Do you remember that time in English class when Father Vaughan made us each choose a poem to memorise?"

"Yes, I picked 'Lochinvar' by Sir Water Scott," said Artie, "you know, about the bold young knight." He cast his mind back and began to recite in a whisper:

> *"O young Lochinvar is come out of the west,*
> *Through all the wide border his steed was the best,*
> *And save his good broadsword he weapons had none—"*

"Yes, yes," Ham interrupted brusquely, "I remember you reciting the whole blessed thing. There's no need to do it again."

Artie was slightly put out at being cut off before the end of the stanza. "So what is it you're talking about?" he demanded.

"Well, I picked Robbie Burns' 'Address to a Haggis'."

"Not a soul in the class was in any way surprised by that, Ham."

"But I looked at a lot of other poems first," Ham continued, "including that one about the Crimean War."

"Right," said Artie, "when our army teamed up with the French to keep the Russians out of those ports on the Black Sea."

"Well, I read that poem about the famous battle, and I'm sure it mentions the Six Hundred. It was 'The Charge of the Light Brigade' by Keats."

"By Alfred Lord Tennyson."

"Fine, have it your way. But I'm sure I remember part of it. It goes something like:

Forward, the Light Brigade!
Was there a man dismayed?"

Ham paused and slipped a hand under his cap to scratch his head. "Something, something...

Theirs not to make reply,
Theirs not to reason why,
Theirs but to do or die…"

When he paused again to recall the next line, a mocking voice came from behind them.

"Into the valley of Death
Rode the six hundred."

The boys swung round with a start and fell back against the damp tombstone. They looked up to see the menacing smirk of Colonel Braxton Dash.

16.

The Enigma of the Russian Cross

The boys scrambled upright and faced the sinister colonel. He loomed over them with a heartless grin on his face, clearly smug that he had crept up on them while they were busy reciting poetry. Behind him the Slogger appeared out of the mist, a shovel gripped in his right hand. In the other hand he held the leash of the great black hound Erebus. The dog gave a growl that sent a shiver down Artie's spine.

Braxton Dash poked the end of his gold-handled cane hard into Artie's chest, pushing him back against the tombstone.

"So what have we here? A pair of junior ghouls?"

Artie lowered his gaze, trying to keep his face in shadow so that the colonel wouldn't recognise him.

"What, nothing to say for yourselves?" Dash turned his attention to Ham and gave him a prod with his stick.

"We were just burying a piece of hair," Ham blurted out.

Artie gaped at him in amazement, wondering if his friend had lost his mind.

"Burying hair?" Dash echoed.

"Yes, my g-granny says it's a sure way to g-get rid of warts," Ham stammered.

"Ham…" Artie began, but there was no stopping his friend.

"You see, you cut off a bit of your hair," the words tumbled uncontrollably from Ham's lips, "and bury it in a graveyard – at midnight if possible, but just so long as it's dark it should still work. So you bury the hair, as I said, and when you wake up in the morning all your warts are gone."

"Much troubled with warts, are you, boy?" Dash drawled.

"Yes, very much so." Ham bobbed his head. "We've buried the hair some place over that way." He waved a vague hand. "So as our business is done, we'll be on our way and let you get on with whatever you're about, because it's certainly no concern of ours."

Braxton Dash squinted at Ham for a few seconds and frowned. "Simple minded," he muttered. He turned back to Artie. "And what about you? Cat got your tongue?"

He placed the end of his cane under Artie's chin and forced him to raise his head. He leaned forward to peer closely at his young prisoner's face.

"I know you, don't I?" There was a menacing edge to his voice. "Last night, I sent you to fetch gin and some other

126

sprat came back with the bottle. I thought at the time there was something out of place about you."

"Excuse me, sir," Ham interrupted, "but he was with me last night. We were studying horoscopes. Did you know there's going to be an eclipse?"

"Quiet!" Dash snapped, cuffing Ham on the side of the head.

Artie's hands curled into fists. "You've no call to treat him like that."

Dash let out a dry chuckle. "Well, well, well. There's trouble in you, boy, isn't there?"

Artie tried to control his temper. It was obvious that he and Ham would be no match for the colonel and the Slogger. And he had no wish to tangle with the black mastiff.

Dash drove the end of his cane against Artie's chest again, pressing him back against the tombstone.

"Yes, you left to fetch the gin, then Warren disappeared right after." He ran a hand across his moustache. "Rather suspicious that."

Out of the corner of his eye Artie could see the look of helpless despair on Ham's face. Perhaps if he could distract the two villains, there might be a chance for his friend to escape.

"I have nothing to say to you," he told the colonel, his face reddening with frustration, "so you might as well let us go."

Dash appeared not to hear. "You and Warren, taking off

together like that," he murmured. "Could it be that you're in league with him, that he's planning a double cross?" He reached out a gloved hand and clamped Artie's jaw between his fingers. "I don't like rascals who double cross me."

Artie could hear Ham panting in panic and his own heart was hammering in his chest. The Slogger dropped the shovel and cracked his knuckles. The noise was as frightening as a pistol shot.

"I've a notion you know a good deal more than you're telling." Dash's fingers dug hard into Artie's cheeks. "If you and your friend want to keep your throats from being cut, I suggest you tell me everything you know about the Russian Cross."

The Russian Cross!

Artie's thoughts reeled. He had no idea what the colonel was talking about. He couldn't even think of a lie that would buy them some time. But it seemed Dr Harthill had been right – this mystery wasn't about the bodies themselves; it was some form of criminal treasure hunt.

Braxton Dash released his grip on Artie's face and tapped him under the jaw with his knuckles. "My patience is wearing very thin, boy. Tell me about the Russian Cross!"

The clues were whirling around in Artie's brain like leaves in a whirlwind. The Six Hundred, the six graves, DC, the Light Brigade charging the Russian guns...

"It comes from the Crimea," he blurted, thoughts flashing

in his brain like the sparks from Dr Harthill's machinery. "The Light Brigade brought it back with them, after the battle, after the charge."

"Yes, yes," said Dash, his eyes glittering with greed. "But did he tell you where it's hidden? Curse you, boy, tell me which is the grave!"

Even though his flesh was crawling with terror, Artie was beginning to see the pattern now. If he could only think of a way to divert Braxton Dash.

Just then an unseen owl hooted loudly in a nearby tree. The huge mastiff Erebus stiffened, its ears pricking up as it turned towards the sound. It let out a deep-throated "Baroo!" and charged off after the bird, dragging the Slogger behind it.

"Slogger, hang onto him, man!" Dash roared, lunging after the pair. "Erebus, heel, drat you! Heel!"

Seizing the chance, Artie grabbed Ham by the shoulder and hauled him down the slope towards the gate. The hound was still baying furiously, chasing the owl.

Ham tripped on a lump in the ground and rolled over several times in the wet grass before coming to a halt at the base of a tombstone. Artie helped him back onto his feet, dragged him along again and demanded, "What on earth was all that nonsense about hair and warts?"

"I was remembering what you said about cannibals," Ham puffed. "You know, making them think you'd caused

129

an eclipse by magic. I thought if I said we were doing magic, they might let us go."

Artie couldn't help grinning. "Well, it was a game effort. Come on, let's get out of here!"

Suddenly the dog fell silent and Braxton Dash cried out, "Slogger, those brats have escaped! Unleash the dog! Erebus, take 'em!"

"Oh my goodness, he's setting the hound on us!" Ham squeaked.

"We could do with a spot of magic right now to get us out of this."

They raced for the exit as fast as their legs would carry them.

The gate appeared out of the mist like the way into some dark fairy land. Artie flung it open and they stumbled out into the street, leaving it to clang shut behind them. There came another jarring crash as the black mastiff flung itself at the metal bars.

"He can't get through!" Artie breathed. "It only opens inwards. Come on!"

He and Ham hurried up the street, pelting blindly through the mist. Suddenly they collided with a wall of solid rock.

"We're at the foot of Calton Hill!" Artie exclaimed. "We can't climb here: it's like a cliff face."

Behind them the gate of the burial ground swung open and slammed shut again with a harsh metallic reverberation.

"Dash has let the hound out," Ham panted. "We can't stop now!"

"Look, steps!" Artie pointed. A broad stone stairway cut right up the hillside and the boys bounded up it two steps at a time. Behind them they could hear the rasping breath of the hound drawing ominously closer.

Artie knew there was no way they could outrun the great beast. Worse than that, he knew that he had dragged Ham into this and if anything were to happen to his friend it would be his fault.

Suddenly he spotted a thick branch that had snapped off an overhanging tree during one of the recent storms. He snatched it and gave Ham a push to keep him staggering up the hill.

"I'll hold it off," he gasped. "You go! Get help if you can!"

Ham stared at him in shock. "Artie, no!"

"Go!" Artie propelled his friend upward with a determined shove. He spun round and saw the black shape of the mastiff charging towards him. A line from the poem about Lochinvar flashed through his mind.

And save his good broadsword he weapons had none.

This branch wasn't much of a broadsword, but then he probably wasn't much of a knight or he wouldn't be so afraid. Gripping the makeshift weapon in both hands, he thrust it out in front of him.

131

The hound was undeterred. With a savage howl it launched itself into the air, coming right down on top of its prey. The branch snapped in two and Artie's back hit the stone steps so hard it knocked the breath out of him.

Pinned beneath the mastiff's massive paws, he felt the blood drain out of his face. Great, slavering jaws hung over him and the monster's lips curled back to expose its vicious fangs.

The Affair of the Crimean Soldier

The mastiff's massive head swung from side to side above Artie, as if the hound were trying to make up its mind whether to rip out his throat or bite off his head. He was so crushed by its weight, he could barely draw breath.

"This way, Slogger!" he heard Colonel Braxton Dash call. "I swear they went this way. Erebus, where are you, you cur?"

"I can't see 'em, Colonel," The Slogger's slow, heavy voice responded.

Artie knew his only choice now was to face his fate bravely like Sir Lancelot, or Sir Galahad, or the great knight Roland who died heroically defending the pass at Roncevalles. With any luck Ham had made a clean getaway and would set the police on the trail of Dash and his Gravediggers.

The last thing he expected was to hear Ham's voice saying coaxingly, "Here, boy. Here's a treat for you."

Artie swivelled his eyes upward. Ham was crouched on one of the steps above him with an aniseed cake in his outstretched hand.

"Here, boy, this is really good. Much tastier than old Artie there."

"Ham, I told you to–"

"Quiet, Artie!" Ham cut him off. He resumed his coaxing tone. "There's a good dog. I bet you'd like a nice treat, wouldn't you?"

The hound stared fixedly at the cake. The growl in its throat softened almost to a purr.

The voices of Colonel Dash and the Slogger drew closer.

"Ham, you need to get away," said Artie in an urgent whisper, "before they catch you."

Ham ignored him. "Here you go, boy," he said to the dog.

He tossed the cake towards the hound. It opened its massive jaws, caught the cake, swished it around in its mouth then swallowed it. It licked its lips and panted approvingly.

Ham reached into his pocket and produced a second cake. "Good boy! See, I've got another one here for you."

The dog rose up from its haunches, lifting its weight from Artie's body so that he could breath again. It stared hungrily at the sweet treat.

"Here, why don't you fetch it?" Ham drew back his arm.

He flung the cake and sent it bouncing down the hill into

the mist. With a gleeful yelp, the mastiff bounded off in pursuit and vanished into the murk.

"Ham, what came over you?" Artie asked in astonishment, as his friend helped him to his feet.

"I'm not sure." Ham shook his head. "I think I had a sudden attack of courage. I hope it doesn't happen again. My knees are shaking."

"Let's get moving." Artie led the way up the stairs.

"I say, you're not going to rag on me for bringing those cakes along, are you?" Ham asked.

"Definitely not," Artie assured him. "Those cakes of yours turned out to be a real life saver. Now let's hope there's a place up there we can hide."

"Boys! Boys!" a voice called urgently. "Come with me!"

Through the mist Artie saw Benjamin Warren standing at the top of the hill, beckoning them on.

"What on earth are you doing here?" Artie demanded.

"Look, will you just follow me," Warren insisted, "before they catch up!"

For a moment a suspicion flickered through Artie's mind that Warren was in league with Braxton Dash and was leading them into a trap. But that made no sense. All he had to do was call out to the two villains to bring them running.

Warren rapidly led the way over the top of Calton Hill and down the grassy slope on the far side.

"I suspected that you'd overheard Dash talking about

135

Calton Burial Ground," he panted, "and would be unable to keep your nose out of it. That's why I decided to keep a watch out for you, but this blessed mist put paid to that."

"Why didn't you show yourself sooner?" asked Ham.

Warren shook his head. "I couldn't risk Dash catching sight of me. He's already suspicious and I can only keep Geraldine safe for as long as he thinks I'm playing along with his scheme."

"Who the dickens is Geraldine?" Ham wondered, sounding more confused than ever.

"I think we're about to find out," said Artie as they reached the bottom of the hill.

Here in Royal Terrace a horse-drawn carriage awaited them. Painted on the side was a shield bearing the images of three thistles and a moorhen. Seated in the carriage was the Lady in Grey. Climbing aboard, Warren hastily introduced the girl as Miss Geraldine Poulton. Artie noticed that under her cloak she was clutching a canvas bag in her small, white fingers. There was just enough room for all of them with Artie and Ham squeezed between Warren and the girl. With a flick of the reins the student started the horse and they trotted off down the road.

When they turned a corner Artie gasped and Ham let out a squeak. Colonel Braxton Dash was charging towards them, brandishing his cane. The Slogger was at his side, hauling the black hound along by its leash.

Muttering an oath, Warren swerved into a side street, away from the two villains.

"Warren, rein in, curse you!" Dash roared, striking his cane against the ground in frustration.

The carriage rushed on, leaving the colonel and his henchman lost in the mist.

"The game's up now," said Warren through gritted teeth.

"We can't go home," the girl pointed out. "He knows where we both live."

"I know a place where we'll be safe," said Artie. "But when we get there, you have to tell us everything."

"I suppose the truth might as well come out now," said Geraldine, "now that we must confront those villains."

"Alright, Arthur," said Warren. "Where are we headed?"

They soon arrived outside Dr Harthill's house in Rutland Square. Warren tethered the horse to the railings while everyone dismounted from the carriage.

"Is that a coat of arms?" Artie asked, looking at the decorative shield painted on its side.

"Yes," Warren replied, "I borrowed the carriage from one of my wealthier classmates, the young Lord Strathairn."

They walked towards the grand front door of Dr Harthill's townhouse.

"You say this friend of yours is a doctor?" asked Geraldine.

The girl seemed weak from lack of food or sleep, but she bore herself bravely.

"I'm sure Dr Harthill can mix you a tonic if you need one," said Artie. "More importantly, he is the cleverest man I know, so if there's a mystery to solve, he can be of enormous help."

"There is certainly a mystery to solve," said Geraldine as they approached the front door, "and I'll be glad of some extra minds to help me thwart that awful man Braxton Dash."

"If we all put our heads together," Warren added, "we may yet crack this problem."

For the first time since they had met, Artie noticed a faint smile on Geraldine's lips.

Artie was ringing the bell for the third time when Dr Harthill opened the door. He peered curiously at his visitors down the length of his nose. He was fully dressed but his tie was loose, his shirt partly unbuttoned, and his long hair disordered.

"Mr Doyle," he said, blinking, "this is a highly unorthodox hour to come calling."

"I'm sorry about that, Dr Harthill, but we desperately need your help. It's to do with the matter of the six stolen corpses. I fear we are in grave danger."

"Indeed!" Harthill's eyebrows shot up in surprise. "Well,

well. Come inside at once. As a medical man, it is my sworn duty to help those in any sort of need."

They followed him down the hallway, where Warren and Geraldine stared curiously at the photographs and anatomical drawings hanging on the walls. The doctor led them into a modestly furnished parlour. Artie and Ham each took a chair while Warren and Geraldine shared a divan. After Artie had made the introductions, Harthill presented Geraldine and Warren each with a glass of sherry then poured two tumblers of elderflower cordial for the boys.

"There," he said, smoothing back his long hair, "that should soothe away the chill of a winter's night."

He settled himself in a comfy armchair and raised his own sherry glass to Benjamin Warren. "A medical student, eh? It is a noble profession, but you must apply yourself, young man – yes, apply yourself."

"I'll be better able to do that, sir," Warren responded, "if we can extricate ourselves from this awful predicament."

"Tell me what you know, and we'll see how I can be of service," said the doctor.

"You were right, Dr Harthill, to suggest that the bodies were a mere distraction for what was really going on." Artie brought their host up to date with the case. "A ghastly criminal gang is at work, searching for a long-lost treasure, something to do with 'the Six Hundred'." He turned his

139

attention to Warren and Geraldine. "Maybe it's time you explained the rest. What is this Russian Cross that Colonel Braxton Dash is searching for?"

"And what has it got to do with the Charge of the Light Brigade?" asked Ham.

Geraldine took a sip of sherry to fortify herself then set the glass aside. "I suppose I should tell the tale." She drew herself up straight. "It is all to do with my father, Francis Poulton, late of the Fourth Light Dragoons."

"In the Crimean War," Warren added, "that regiment was part of the famed Light Brigade."

"For many years my father suffered ill health because of the wounds he received at the Battle of Balaclava," said Geraldine. "Then just last week he… he…" Her voice faltered and her eyes dropped to the canvas bag in her lap.

Warren interposed, squeezing her hand to comfort her. "Last week Mr Poulton passed away, leaving behind him only a few clues to the location of a treasure he brought back with him from the Crimea some eighteen years ago."

Geraldine looked up and Dr Harthill gestured at her to continue. She opened the canvas bag and pulled out several loose pages covered in elegant handwriting.

"The story is here," she said, "dictated to me during the last few days of my father's life." As she gazed at the manuscript, tears glinted in her deep grey eyes.

"Perhaps, my dear, I should read that out," Dr Harthill suggested, leaning forward to take the pages from her.

"Yes, if you would," the girl gratefully agreed.

The doctor settled back in his armchair with the manuscript in his hand. He slipped on his reading glasses and moved them up and down his long nose until the page came into focus. Then he cleared his throat and began to read aloud.

18.

The Tale of the Four Companions

Dictated by me, Francis Poulton, to my daughter, Geraldine Poulton, this January, in the Year of Our Lord 1872.

I fear I have but a short span of life remaining to me, and that soon I will be joining my dear wife Martha. I will be better fitted to face the Lord's judgement if I make a clean breast of the whole matter of the Russian Cross and of the crime that brought it into my hands.

There were the four of us cavalrymen who had become fast friends and constant companions since joining the Fourth Light Dragoons: John Evermore, Dennis Hayes, Marcus Brand and myself. We were a rowdy crew to be sure, indulging overmuch in beer and gambling. While none of us was what I would call a virtuous man, Marcus

Brand was the worst, for there was in him a streak of genuine cruelty that went beyond the careless high spirits of youth.

In 1854 we and our horses were shipped out to the Crimea where our regiment formed part of the Light Brigade. Along with our French allies, we were there to assist the Turks in their war with the Russians. It was our aim to prevent the Russians from taking control of the Black Sea, and thus gaining access to the Mediterranean.

A hard time we had of it, what with the bad weather, the poor rations and the constant thunder of artillery on both sides. Our enemy was more ferocious than we'd been led to expect, and our allies less dependable. Our forces were gathered at Balaclava to block the Russian advance and it is here that my story begins.

The four of us were often sent out together on scouting missions. On one such occasion we came upon a gaudily clad Russian officer watering his horse at a stream. Dismounted as he was, we caught him unawares and made him our prisoner. He barely looked old enough to shave, but from his finery, he was clearly of high rank.

His name, he told us, was Prince Alexei, a cousin and favourite of Tsar Nicholas, the ruler of Russia. He pleaded for his freedom and brought out from under his shirt a fabulous jewelled cross as big as your hand. Solid gold it was and studded with rubies and emeralds. Encased inside the cross was the finger bone of some Russian

143

saint, and the Tsar had gifted him this holy relic to keep him safe amid the dangers of war.

He offered to give us this treasure if we would only set him free to return to his own lines. We accepted the deal and Evermore took the cross from him. But then, as the Russian turned to leave, Brand levelled his pistol at him and shot him dead.

The rest of us were outraged by this ignoble act, but Brand pointed out that the only way we could keep the cross for ourselves was if nobody else knew we possessed it. If our own generals knew of it, they would take it for themselves. When the war was over neither Queen nor country would have any care for our welfare, but the profit we made from selling the gold and jewels would keep us all in comfort for years.

Ashamed as we were of how the matter had turned out, none of us was going to refuse his part of the treasure. We buried it together behind a ruined mill on the edge of our encampment and all swore an oath of secrecy. However, even as we returned to camp, I felt in my heart a dark presentiment that no good would come of it.

Next day, battle broke out in earnest – the Battle of Balaclava it was called in the newspapers, which reported very fully the dreadful events. As infantrymen swarmed over the hills on either side of us and cannon thundered across the valley, we of the Light Brigade awaited the order that would tell us where to strike.

When that order came there appeared to be some confusion among our officers. We were to charge the guns, but which guns nobody had made clear. It was Captain Nolan of the 15th Hussars who drew his sword and pointed to the Russian artillery positioned at the far end of the valley.

"There is your enemy!" he declared. "There are your guns!"

All down our line, trumpets sounded the advance and forward went the Light Brigade. Who has not heard that tale of tragedy and courage? Mr Tennyson wrote truly when he said in his famous poem that there were cannon to the right of us, cannon to the left of us, and we were riding into the Valley of Death.

The Russian guns blazed all around us, bringing down men and horses as we thundered on. Captain Nolan himself was one of the first to fall. Of over six hundred of us who made the charge, barely fifty reached the end of the valley. Then they had to turn back or risk being surrounded by enemy cavalry. My horse was shot out from under me, and in the chaos and confusion, I staggered back towards our lines on foot. A shell exploded at my back, knocking me to the ground, unconscious.

Some of my comrades must have carried me the rest of the way, for when I awoke I lay in a cot in the hospital tent, surrounded by the groans of the wounded and the dying. My leg had been broken and was bound with a splint, and I had taken a piece of shrapnel in my head that pained me for the rest of my days.

I learned that Brand and Hayes had both died in the charge, while Evermore was in a cot not far from mine. He was so badly injured that he was half out of his mind and not expected to live through the night. As I lay there, I could not shake off the notion that the murder of the prince and the theft of the cross had brought down a curse, not only on the four of us, but on the whole of the Light Brigade.

Poor Evermore was running a fever and his mouth was running off too. "The cross," I heard him rant, "it was the cross that done it. Oh, if only we had never set eyes on it!"

I limped painfully over to his cot and tried to calm him. "Hush there, Johnny," I told him. "You mustn't speak of that."

I touched a finger to his lips to quiet him and realised at once that his breath had stopped.

Of the four of us I was the only survivor. I gazed warily around me. What thoughtless words of his had been heard among the wounded and the medical staff? Might he in his delirium have given away the location of the cross?

That night, in spite of the agony of my wounds, I made my way in secret to the hiding place and dug up the jewelled cross. I wrapped it in a linen cloth and hid it in my pack beneath my shaving kit. As I was no longer fit to fight, I was shipped back to England some weeks later, there to rejoin my dear wife Martha and our infant daughter Geraldine.

In subsequent years I heard rumours spreading among the veterans of the Crimea. On the eve of Balaclava, it was said, a Russian prince had been robbed and killed for a golden cross worth a small fortune. There was speculation that it had fallen into the hands of some British soldiers and was even now concealed somewhere in these isles.

Whether Evermore's feverish ranting had given rise to these rumours, or whether one of the others had foolishly let slip the tale before the battle, I could not know. But my great fear was that someone would connect the cross to Brand, and Brand to me. So I moved my family from place to place to elude any who might seek me out, taking care at all times to keep the cross hidden.

Finally we settled in Edinburgh a little over two years ago, shortly after which my poor wife died. As my health declined, I pondered what I should do with this cursed treasure. To turn it to my own profit would, I was sure, bring more ill fortune down upon our heads, but I could not leave the cursed treasure in your hands, dearest Geraldine.

At last I concealed it in the earth at the foot of an open grave, mere hours before the funeral party arrived to bury a coffin on top of it. There it lies in the place of my brethren under the mark of DC, in honour of the Six Hundred, as Tennyson famously called them.

It is my prayer that should it be found, the cross will be used to help the survivors of that terrible charge. Many of them, like me, were badly wounded and have fallen into poverty. Some have been driven into the workhouse, while others have been compelled to turn beggar. Perhaps one day the Russian Cross can be used to bring them some comfort and dignity in their final years.

This is a true testimony, as God is my witness. And now that I face the final night of my soul, I pray for His mercy and forgiveness.

Francis Poulton,
Late of the Fourth Light Dragoons

19.

The Doctor Makes a Deduction

Once he had finished reading Francis Poulton's narrative, Dr Harthill removed his glasses and rubbed his eyes.

"A remarkable tale," he declared. "Remarkable."

"Artie, you were right about the DC being Roman numerals," said Ham.

"And you were right about that pointing to the Light Brigade," said Artie.

Geraldine Poulton's eyes had been downcast throughout the reading, but now she looked up and took a deep breath to steady herself against her grief.

"Though skilled in the care of horses," she said, "my father found it difficult to retain employment As well as being lame in one leg, the headaches he suffered were often so severe that they robbed him of his wits. My mother earned what she could as a seamstress and by taking in laundry, and as soon as I was old enough to assist her, I took up my share."

"It's not right that men who have fought for their country should be forced to live in such a way," said Artie. He knew only too well the difficulties a family faced when the father struggled with ill health, and he had every sympathy for Geraldine's circumstances. For a moment his mind was clouded with foreboding over the future of his own family.

"Such, I am afraid, is the way of the world," Dr Harthill commented sadly.

"As you've heard," Geraldine continued, "we moved frequently from place to place, though I did not know the reason why. When my mother died nearly two years ago, the care of my father fell to me. For the last weeks of his life he was bedridden."

The painful memory made the girl pause and Warren took the opportunity to add his part of the story.

"It was at the pharmacy that I first met Geraldine," he said. "She was buying medicine to soothe her father's headaches and could barely muster the price. From her conversation with the pharmacist I gathered that she could not afford the services of a doctor, so I offered to assist."

"Benjamin has been kindness itself." Geraldine smiled at the student. "Coming by whenever he could to minister to my poor sick father."

"I obtained some laudanum to alleviate his pain," said Warren, "and it was while under the influence of the drug that he began to tell us about the precious relic he had brought back from the Crimea."

"He made frequent reference to its being buried under the mark of DC," Geraldine added.

"And how did this villainous Colonel Braxton Dash become involved?" inquired Dr Harthill, frowning.

"That was my fault," Warren admitted with a grim shake of the head.

Artie could tell by his unhappy expression just how ashamed he felt.

Geraldine laid a gentle hand on the medical student's shoulder. "Benjamin, you have nothing to reproach yourself with. It was an accident of circumstance."

"I was spending an evening at a gambling house with a group of my fellow students, as well as some less reputable company," Warren recalled. "Wine had loosened my tongue to the point where I mentioned that I had a patient under my care who was a veteran of the Light Brigade. I even let slip his name, Francis Poulton. Somehow Braxton Dash overheard. He drew me aside, shared a bottle of whisky with me, and lured me into an expensive card game. By the end of the night I owed him more money than I could possibly repay."

"No doubt he has all manner of tricks for cheating at cards," said Geraldine.

"I know that now," said Warren ruefully. "Anyway, Dash made light of the debt and told me I could pay it off with a small favour. It seemed an uncle of his who had served in the Crimea had told Dash the rumour of the stolen cross and mentioned the names of some who were suspected of the crime. He asked if Poulton had ever mentioned such a thing, and I'm ashamed to say that I told him I had heard him talk of it." He threw back the last of his sherry and set down the empty glass.

"He pressed me to bring him every scrap of information I could obtain concerning the hiding place of the treasure," said Warren. "He was sure that while the invalid was under my care, he would let slip the secret sooner or later."

"Benjamin confessed his mistake to me from the start," said Geraldine. "My greatest fear was that Dash and his henchmen would break into our house and try to obtain the information by force."

"That was why I shared only enough of the story to convince him to leave the task to me," said Warren. "First I told him that it was buried in a grave, for that would be of little help. Eventually I let him know about the mark of DC, for we ourselves could make little sense of this."

"I would imagine that the number of gravestone inscriptions containing those letters must be beyond counting," said Geraldine.

"Not so many as you think," said Artie. "The graves he

152

had dug up all featured the letters D and C as capitals and in that order."

"Yes, Dash became impatient waiting for more information," said Warren, "so he began his search for the cross using only those clues."

"What I don't understand," said Ham, "is why didn't he just leave the bodies by the graveside? Why go to all the bother of carting them away?"

"As I explained to you on your previous visit, Mr Hamilton," Dr Harthill steepled his fingers thoughtfully under his chin, "it was most likely a matter of misdirection."

"Dash doesn't want anyone to suspect what he's really up to," Artie explained.

"When Mr Poulton passed away," said Warren, "it was all I could do to keep Dash from kidnapping Geraldine to force more information from her. I persuaded him to let me continue working with her in attempting to locate the cross. But he has been pressing me hard."

"I assume that night you came dashing into the house out of the fog, you were escaping an encounter with him?" asked Artie.

"Yes, I was supposed to meet Geraldine at Greyfriars that night so we could search together," said Warren, "but one of my lecturers, Dr Bell, made me stay late to help him inventory his lab equipment. By the time I arrived Geraldine had entered the graveyard without me."

"As soon as I heard voices I took to be Colonal Dash and his henchman, I regretted my impatience," said Geraldine. "I escaped the graveyard and fled down the street where I ran into Ben as he was coming to find me."

"I escorted Geraldine home," said Warren, "but as soon as I left her, Dash waylaid me and pressed me for what I had learned. I managed to lose him in the fog and ran off in a bit of a panic."

"Benjamin and I have visited various cemeteries around the city," said Geraldine, "hoping to spy some definite clue to the hiding place of the cross."

"Our intention was to find it ourselves before Dash can get his hands on it," said Warren.

"But we can't even fathom out which graveyard my father alluded to." Geraldine sounded frustrated. "Perhaps you kind gentlemen can help us solve this mystery?"

"I believe, now we have all the information to hand, that we can," said Artie resolutely. "Didn't he say, It lies in the place of my brethren?"

Professor Harthill slipped his glasses back on and scrutinised the last page of the manuscript. "Yes, that is correct."

"But that makes no sense at all," said Geraldine. "My father had no brothers or sisters that I know of."

"Might he have been talking about his fellow soldiers?" Ham suggested.

"I did think of that," said Warren, "but there is no graveyard in Edinburgh set aside specifically for soldiers."

"I may be able to shed some light on this." Dr Harthill removed his glasses and tapped the manuscript with his forefinger. "Tell me, Miss Poulton, was your father a religious man?"

"In his later years," Geraldine replied, "he did wonder what fate might await him beyond the grave. He gained much comfort from reading *The Lives of the Saints* and his last words to me as he passed away were, 'God is love'."

Dr Harthill clapped his hands gleefully and said, "The saints! Of course!"

Ham leaned close to Artie and whispered, "The old chap's acting very peculiarly. Do you think all that electricity has affected his brain?"

"No, Ham, I think he's just deduced something very important."

"I have indeed, my young friend, I have indeed," Dr Harthill confirmed with a beaming smile. "I can tell you where the grave in question is to be found. It is elementary, my dear boy."

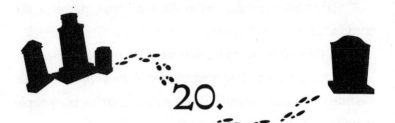

20.

The Finding of the Final Grave

"I believe I have deduced which burial ground you should be searching," proclaimed Dr Harthill.

"The 'place of my brethren', you mean?" said Artie.

"Precisely," said Dr Harthill. "Miss Poulton, you stated that in his latter years your father took comfort in reading *The Lives of the Saints*."

Geraldine looked bewildered. "Yes, but how does that help us?"

"Your father's name was Francis," said the doctor, "which is the name of one of the most famous saints in all of history."

"St Francis of Assisi," said Artie.

"Quite correct, Mr Doyle," the doctor complimented him.

"Maybe I haven't studied my saints hard enough," said Ham, "but I'm still not seeing any light in this."

"St Francis formed a religious brotherhood," said the doctor, "an order of monks."

"Yes, they were called Franciscans," said Artie.

"Quite," Dr Harthill agreed. "But they had another name. Because of the distinctive grey robes they wore, people commonly referred to them as the Grey Friars."

"The Grey Friars!" Artie gasped. "Of course, Greyfriars Kirkyard!"

"I did find myself drawn to that particular kirkyard," said Geraldine. "Which is why I was so determined to visit that time, even so late at night."

"Hmm, yes, the clue your father left was working in the deepest part of your psyche," Doctor Harthill theorised, "prompting you to visit that place. Now that the knowledge is at the forefront of your brain, you may act more decisively."

"Yes, we must!" Warren jumped to his feet. "Now Dash knows that I am working against him, he will pursue us with all the resources at his command."

He offered Geraldine his hand and drew her to her feet.

"We must start our search immediately," she said, "and pray that we are guided to our goal."

Artie got up and stood by Warren's side. "Dash has already dug up two DC graves at Greyfriars. With any luck we can find the right one before he overtakes us."

Ham looked deeply unhappy at the prospect of another

night in a graveyard. He rubbed his hands on his knees, as though trying to coax himself into movement.

"Yes." He forced himself up and out of his chair. "We must see this business through to the end."

"Well said, Ham," said Artie proudly.

"You'll need the correct equipment," said Dr Harthill. "My gardener keeps a pair of shovels at the back of the house and I can loan you some electrical lanterns."

"Electrical lanterns?" said Ham suspiciously. "They won't fry us or anything, will they?"

"Not at all, Mr Hamilton," the doctor chortled. "They are the very newest thing."

Carrying the equipment provided, they returned to the carriage. Harthill wished them good luck from his open doorway as they clambered aboard. Warren was flicking the reins to set the horse in motion when Artie suddenly started in his seat.

"What is it, Artie?" Ham asked. "What's wrong?"

"Oh, nothing, Ham." Artie quickly regained his composure. "Nothing important."

Artie didn't wish to cause alarm, but he could swear he had glimpsed someone watching them from the fog-shrouded square – a shadowy figure hiding in the darkness. He touched a finger to his lips to signal Ham to say no more about it as they drove off through the murky, benighted streets.

By the time they reached Greyfriars Kirkyard, there was a determined gleam in Geraldine's eyes.

"Are you sure you're ready for this?" Warren asked as he helped her down from the carriage.

"I am fixed in my purpose," she answered with her head held high. "I will rescue my father's honour and be daunted by nothing."

Her courage brought an admiring smile to the young man's face.

While Warren and Ham carried the shovels, Artie and Geraldine each held one of Dr Harthill's lanterns. Following the doctor's instructions, they rapidly wound the handle at the base of each lantern until the tube inside lit up with a bluish white fluorescence.

With this light to guide them, they passed through the gate into the damp, grey kirkyard.

"What puzzles me," said Ham, wrinkling his nose, "is why old Mr Poulton didn't just come out and say, 'Listen, my dear, here's where I buried the blessed thing. You go and dig it up whenever you think the time is right.' Why be so mysterious?"

"Through the years," said Geraldine, "perhaps because of his guilt over what happened in the Crimea, he became more and more secretive."

"Also," said Warren, "he was deathly afraid of the cross falling into the wrong hands. This way, only someone who knew him well could even attempt to follow the subtle clues he left behind."

"Well, it's going to be a hard search." Ham gazed out at the rows of gravestones. "The letters DC don't exactly leap out at you, even in daylight."

"Then we had best begin at once," said Geraldine decisively. "We should form two parties and examine the names on the graves as swiftly as we can."

"Just a moment," said Artie as they started up the path. "We may have been going about this all wrong."

Everyone turned to face him as he rubbed his brow in concentration.

"What do you mean, Arthur?" asked Warren.

"Well, we've been assuming the letters D and C formed part of the name of some deceased person," said Artie.

"How could they be anything else?" Geraldine frowned.

"The last words your father spoke to you, what were they again?" Artie asked.

"He told me, 'God is love'. He was trying to comfort me in my grief."

"I don't think so," said Artie thoughtfully. "I think he was giving you the final clue you needed to find the cross."

"Artie, you've lost me completely – again," sighed Ham.

"Remember your Latin." Artie was certain now that he

had the truth of it. "God is love in Latin would be Deus Caritas."

"DC!" Warren exclaimed. "Why, yes, it makes perfect sense."

"Now, only a few of the gravestones here have Latin inscriptions," said Artie, "and I'll bet only one has those exact words."

"Oh, let that be the case!" Geraldine's eyes were bright with excitement. "Quickly, let's delay no longer!"

There was a large area to cover, but with the brilliant light of Dr Harthill's electrical lanterns to guide them, they were soon gathered in front of a stone:

HERE LIES

RODERICK TULLOCH

1809–1871

BELOVED HUSBAND
AND FATHER

DEUS CARITAS

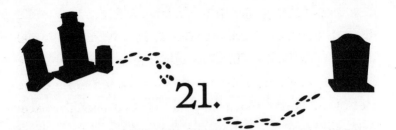

The Honour of
the Light Brigade

"Now that we've finally found the right grave," said Geraldine, "I feel uneasy about disturbing this poor man's place of rest."

"We shall disturb Mr Tulloch as little as possible," Warren assured her, "and we shall see him decently covered up again before we depart."

Artie thought of the shadowy figure they had spotted spying on them when they left Dr Harthill's house.

"We had best get started." He took the shovel from Ham and passed him the lantern. "There's no telling when Braxton Dash may catch up with us."

"Right, Arthur, you and I will commence digging," said Warren. "Geraldine, you and Ham keep a lookout for anyone approaching."

Warren did most of the digging while Artie and Ham

took turns helping him. It was a long, arduous task to dig through the frozen ground, but at last Warren's shovel struck the coffin lid. The closeness of their goal gave Artie and him renewed energy as they excavated around the foot of the coffin. Once they had cleared enough space, Artie squeezed down between the coffin and the side of the hole.

"Careful there, Arthur," Warren cautioned, handing Artie a small trowel, which also came from the store of Dr Harthill's gardener.

Pressing himself down as far as he could, Artie pushed the trowel under the foot of the coffin and used it to loosen the earth.

"There is something here," he reported excitedly. "I can feel the point of the trowel bumping against it."

His three companions leaned over to watch, their lanterns held high, while he forced his arm through the loosened earth beneath the coffin. His heart hammered with excitement as the tips of his fingers touched an object wrapped in cloth. Pushing his arm in as far as it would go, he closed his hand around his discovery and dragged it out.

It was a piece of dirt-smudged linen wrapped around a cruciform shape nearly as long as his forearm. He hoisted it aloft with a hoarse laugh that was both exhausted and triumphant. Warren gripped his other hand and hauled him up out of the grave.

Artie stood before them, his face and clothes caked with dirt, his find laid across the flat of his hands.

"Artie, it can't be really, can it?" Ham breathed in astonishment.

"I don't know, Ham." Artie stared at the dirty linen wrapping. "I can hardly believe it myself."

"Geraldine, you should do the honours," said Warren. "After all, it belongs to you now."

Geraldine stretched out a tentative hand towards the object. "I can hardly bring myself to do it." Her voice trembled with emotion.

Delicately, as though the treasure inside might break, she peeled back the folds of the linen covering. All four of them gaped as she lifted up a magnificent cross of pure, shining gold. Down its length and across its arms, rubies and emeralds flared like stars under the brilliance of the electrical lanterns.

Artie let out a whoop of sheer elation and everyone laughed.

But their joy was cut brutally short by a ghastly howl that echoed across the churchyard.

Aaaahrooooo!

"The hound!" Artie gasped in horror.

Geraldine clutched the cross tightly as the black mastiff came bounding out of the mist towards them, howling like a vengeful spirit. It ran around behind them and stood there growling, daring them to make a move.

From the other side of the grave, Colonel Braxton Dash stepped out of the shadows with the Slogger close on his heels.

"I'm very pleased to make your acquaintance at last, Miss Poulton," he said.

"I take no pleasure from the meeting," Geraldine retorted sharply, "and there shall be no satisfaction in it for you."

Two more of Dash's men emerged from the shadows: one with a black beard and an eyepatch, the other a crafty-looking weasel of a fellow. They spread out, surrounding the party at the graveside. Behind them the hound gave a warning growl to keep them from retreating.

"You really should have chosen a less conspicuous means of transport," the colonel drawled. "All I had to do was promise a guinea's reward to anyone who brought me word of a carriage bearing that particular coat of arms."

He and the Slogger began to make their way around the open grave, the colonel's eyes fixed greedily on the jewelled cross.

"Keep your distance, Dash," Warren warned. "I'm done with you and your schemes."

"You forget that you are in my debt," Dash reminded

him, "not only because of the money you owe, but because I generously allowed you to continue your dalliance with this young flower. Hand over the cross now, and I'll consider both debts cancelled. Otherwise, I promise that the future for both of you will not be rosy."

"That cross belongs to the soldiers who served in the Crimea," Artie defied him, "not to a fraud like you."

"Fraud, is it?" Dash snarled angrily. "Those who fall foul of me find me real enough, as you are about to learn. Slogger, fetch me that trinket! And don't bother to be gentle about it."

The moment the Slogger took a step towards Geraldine, Warren raised his shovel and swung it at him. The boxer caught the handle in his beefy hand and used it to yank the young student into range of his fist. One hammering blow to the stomach knocked the breath out of Warren and left him doubled up on the ground, gasping painfully like a fish thrown out of the water.

Geraldine and Ham pressed together for protection as the other two henchmen and the great hound blocked off any escape. Artie realised he was the only one standing between them and the advancing Slogger. He would sooner have faced a dragon than the giant boxer, but he raised his fists and took up a fighting stance as he had seen in a manual of fisticuffs.

"Let's have you then," he challenged. "You'll not trick me as you did Dancing Donny."

The Slogger's face contorted in a mixture of surprise and puzzlement that a mere boy should have the nerve to confront him.

Colonel Braxton Dash let out a harsh, contemptuous laugh. "Beat him into a pulp, Slogger," he ordered, "then we can get back to business."

The Slogger took a swing, but Artie ducked under his fist and landed a jab at the big man's belly. The blow was too light to hurt the boxer but it angered him.

"Why, you little worm," he rumbled. "I'll knock you clear out of your skin."

He took another swing but Artie again avoided it. The boxer was not used to so small a target. Artie concentrated all his attention on drawing his opponent forward while staying alert to his surroundings.

"I don't think you can beat anybody without your master pulling a cheat for you," he taunted the big man. "I've seen snowmen move faster than you."

"I'll show you how fast I can be!" the Slogger roared, lunging forward behind an outstretched fist.

At that precise instant Artie threw himself to the ground right at his opponent's feet. Carried forward by his own momentum, the enraged Slogger tripped over him and toppled headlong into the open grave, landing with a crash on top of the coffin.

Artie jumped up, but the man with the eyepatch

immediately seized him from behind, trapping his arms against his sides. The weasel-faced man caught hold of Geraldine and tried to prise the jewelled cross from her hands.

"Ham, take the cross and run!" yelled Artie, struggling in the grip of his captor.

Geraldine let Ham pull the cross from her grasp, then seized onto Weasel-Face to keep him from chasing the boy.

Dash chased after the treasure, and as he passed the open grave commanded, "Get out of there, Slogger!"

Clutching the cross in both hands, Ham tried to run, but found his way blocked by the great mastiff. The dog was not growling, however. Its tongue lolled out and it settled back on its haunches with one paw upraised, as if begging.

"I'm s-sorry, boy," Ham stammered, suddenly understanding what the beast wanted. "I'm afraid I'm completely out of cakes."

In a few quick strides Braxton Dash closed the distance between them. He grabbed Ham by the shoulder and spun him round.

"I'll have that cross off you now," he snarled.

Ham's face was white with fear but he tightened his grip on the treasure and set his jaw.

"You shan't have it," he stated defiantly.

"You miserable pup!" snapped Dash. He raised his gold-handled cane and dealt Ham a vicious crack on the side of the head.

With a cry of pain Ham crumpled to the ground. Artie watched helplessly as Dash raised the cane to strike again, but then something extraordinary happened.

The great mastiff let out an angry, booming bark, and launched itself at its master. Braxton Dash was caught completely by surprise and thrown flat on his back. The cane dropped from his startled fingers and rolled away across the grass.

"Drat you, Erebus!" he cursed. "Get off me, you mangy animal!"

He tried to rise, but the dog pinned him down under its massive paws, baring it sharp teeth in a menacing snarl. Dash went still, numb with terror, as the beast's fearsome jaws hovered inches above his throat.

The colonel's henchmen were momentarily taken aback. Seizing his chance, Artie broke loose of Eyepatch's grip and darted to his friend's side. "Ham, are you alright?" he asked anxiously, crouching over him.

Ham groaned. "I feel a bit peaky actually." He was still holding on tightly to the Russian Cross.

"I think you've made yourself a friend." Artie glanced over to where the huge dog was holding Dash prisoner.

"Don't just stand there!" the colonel ordered his men in a choked voice. "Help me!"

The Slogger, who had climbed out of the grave by this time, moved to assist his leader, but a warning growl from

169

the mastiff made him freeze in his tracks. While Weasel-Face wavered indecisively, Geraldine hurried to Warren's side and helped him stagger to his feet.

It was then that a shrill chorus of police whistles pierced the air.

Out of the mist came Lieutenant Sneddon, accompanied by McCorkle and two other constables, brandishing lanterns and waving their truncheons.

"Stand where you are!" yelled Sneddon. "Edinburgh Constabulary!"

At the sight of the police, Weasel-Face and Eyepatch took to their heels and vanished into the darkness. Still shaken from his fall into the grave, the Slogger merely stood with his fists clenched at his sides while the officers surrounded him and his chief.

Handing the jewelled cross over to Geraldine, Ham approached the great hound, which was still standing guard over Braxton Dash. The colonel was seething over his defeat, but dared not move.

Ham reached out hesitantly and patted the dog's huge head. "There now, boy," he said soothingly. "You can let him up now."

The dog abandoned its prisoner, opened its great maw and licked Ham three times across the face.

"Berrybus," Ham laughed, "you're getting me all wet!"

"I believe his name is Erebus," said Artie.

"I think Berrybus suits him better." Ham gave the dog a friendly scratch behind the ear. "Don't you agree, old Berrybus?"

The dog responded by panting happily in Ham's face.

"Dr Harthill!" Artie exclaimed as his friend appeared, hurrying after the constables. "It was you that fetched the police."

"Indeed, Mr Doyle," said the doctor. "As you pulled away in your carriage I saw a suspicious-looking character spying on you. I reasoned that the villain Dash must have sent his minions to track you down, so I deemed it wise to summon the authorities." He nodded approvingly as Lieutenant Sneddon and the constables placed the colonel and the Slogger under arrest. Dash glowered balefully at the two boys as he was led off into custody.

"Thank you, sir, for all your help," said Artie. "As you can see, we've completed our quest."

"You have, you have," Harthill congratulated him with a smile. "And from the signs of struggle, I perceive that you had yourselves quite a battle."

"We did, sir," Artie agreed. "It was a battle for the honour of the Light Brigade."

22.

The Arrival of
a Noble Visitor

Wednesday, January 24, 1872

*Hurrah! The mystery is solved, the villains
arrested, and we are all safe. However, Dr
Harthill says there is one further piece of
business to be settled and has invited us all
to tea at his house.*

Mrs Doyle tugged at Artie's jacket to straighten it then
stepped back to inspect him.

"Yes, you'll do for polite company now," she decided. "But be careful to keep clear of all the muck and soot out there."

"Yes, yes, I'll be very careful," Artie agreed impatiently. "Can I go now? Ham will be waiting for me."

He started for the door but his mother called him back sharply. "One more thing, young man. A fresh handkerchief."

She neatly folded a cotton handkerchief and placed it carefully in his breast pocket. "If you're visiting a doctor, you must look your best. I assume that Benjamin is invited also."

"Yes, I expect so." Artie edged towards the door, only for his mother to pull him back by the elbow and begin adjusting his collar and tie.

"I am so glad you two are getting on now," she said.

"Yes, he's not such a bad fellow, once you get to know him." It had been two days since they had faced Colonel Braxton Dash together at Greyfriars, and being comrades in battle had given Artie a different view of the young student.

"I still don't understand what all this business has been about," Mrs Doyle tutted. "When that officious little man Lieutenant Sneddon brought you back from the Police Office, he said you had assisted him with his inquiries, but the details must remain confidential."

"There are diplomatic complications, I think he called them."

"Well, if you ask me, he's just trying to puff himself up into somebody far more important than he actually is," said Mrs Doyle scornfully.

Before Artie could make it to the door a voice called out, "Arthur, before you go you must see this!"

Charles Doyle emerged from his room carrying a watercolour painting before him like a trophy.

"It's finished at last," he declared. "My painting of Sir Lancelot's castle of Joyous Garde."

The completed painting showed a tall, slender castle of pure white marble rising loftily above the earth as though it had been woven out of gossamer and candlelight. Waving green trees and flights of doves surrounded it, while a golden sun shone down on the scene out of a flawless blue sky.

"Why, Charles, that is splendid!" Mrs Doyle exclaimed in delight.

Artie hardly knew what to say. It was the first painting his father had completed in weeks and it was one of the most beautiful things he had ever seen. "Father, it's like a vision of summer."

Charles Doyle smiled and some trace of colour returned to his pale cheeks. "Yes, I rather fancy the weather has taken a warmer turn. In fact, I think I am well enough to return to the office tomorrow. I expect they've got into rather a mess without me."

Artie felt an impulse to embrace his father, to encourage this rekindling of his spirit, but he was afraid of damaging the painting.

"I think that belongs in a gallery," he said instead. "I'm sure it's only a matter of time."

"Well, off you go then." His mother ushered him towards the door. "You mustn't keep dawdling when there's company waiting for you."

Half an hour later Artie, Ham, Warren and Geraldine were gathered for afternoon tea in Dr Harthill's parlour. Also present was Berrybus, as the great hound was now named, who occupied a large stretch of carpet beside Ham's chair. They sipped their Darjeeling tea and sampled some freshly baked shortbread while the doctor related the latest news of Colonel Braxton Dash.

"The villain Dash has somehow escaped police custody and appears to have vanished from the face of the earth," he reported with an unhappy frown. "It is a most vexing development."

"My guess is that he's fled to Glasgow or Aberdeen or somewhere else where his face isn't known, so that he can adopt a new identity," Warren speculated. "I don't think we'll see him around here again any time soon."

"I should hope not," Geraldine added. "But I'm glad we no longer have any secrets he might be after."

"I still can't believe that after all we've been through, the police took possession of the Russian Cross." Artie expressed his frustration by biting off a large piece of shortbread and crunching on it furiously.

"To be fair," said Geraldine resignedly, "it is technically stolen property."

"And I think we're lucky they didn't arrest us for digging up that grave," said Ham.

Berrybus let out a loud *Gruff!* as if in agreement with his new master.

"And how is your canine lodger settling into his new home, Mr Hamilton?" Dr Harthill asked.

"Oh splendidly," Ham beamed. "I don't think that bogus colonel treated him very well at all."

"How does you mother feel about sharing her home with this new member of the family?" asked Artie.

"She's taken it very well. There have been some burglaries in the neighbourhood, so she's glad to have a dog there to guard the house." He slipped a piece of shortbread to his pet, who munched it down happily.

"Yes, I don't think any burglars would want to tangle with Berrybus," said Artie.

"Well, if no other good comes of all this," said Geraldine, "there is that at least."

"It was very kind of you to invite us all here today, sir," said Artie. "Ham and I are off on the train back to school tomorrow, so I suppose this is as close as we'll get to a victory celebration."

"Kindness wasn't my only motive," said Dr Harthill, rising from his chair as the front doorbell rang. "There is one more part of this adventure yet to be settled."

He disappeared down the hallway and returned with two visitors. One was Constable George McCorkle, looking very official in a freshly pressed uniform. The other was a tall, portly gentleman in an astrakhan coat and a top hat made from felted beaver fur. The stranger fixed a monocle to his right eye as everyone rose to greet him.

"Ladies and gentlemen," said Dr Harthill, "I have the honour to present Count Rostov, the Russian ambassador to the court of Her Majesty Queen Victoria."

The Russian acknowledged the introduction with a small bow.

"The authorities contacted the ambassador by telegram," McCorkle explained, "to inform him that, thanks to the strenuous efforts of the Edinburgh Constabulary, with a little help from certain quarters, a valuable property has been recovered, which belongs by rights to the Russian royal family."

Dr Harthill introduced each of the party in turn to the count, who shook hands with Warren and the boys and bowed low to Geraldine before kissing the back of her hand.

"On behalf of my government," he said in a thick Russian accent, "I thank you all for your efforts in recovering the Cross of St Demetrius, as it is properly called. When the cross went missing during the unfortunate conflict between our countries in the Crimea, the Tsar Nicholas offered a substantial reward for its safe return. Though many years have passed, our present Tsar Alexander fully intends to honour that commitment."

So saying, he reached inside his coat and brought out a large stack of bank notes, which he laid on the table between the teapot and the cake stand.

Geraldine stared at the money uncertainly. "I suppose," she said, "everyone here is entitled to a share."

"A knight doesn't ask a reward for helping a fair lady," Artie told her proudly.

"I already have my reward," said Ham, patting Berrybus's huge head.

"In that case," said Geraldine, "if you feel the same way, Ben..."

Warren smiled at the girl and nodded.

"In that case," she continued, "I will honour my father's final wish and use this money to benefit the survivors of the Light Brigade."

"Well said, Miss Poulton," Dr Harthill proclaimed. "There is more than enough here to create a charitable fund to aid those veterans who have fallen upon hard times."

Ham stared at Artie, who was deep in thought. "What's going through your mind, Artie?" he asked. "When you have that pondering look on your face, it usually means trouble."

"No, not this time, Ham," Artie laughed. "I was just thinking that even the most trying of times can sometimes end happily, just like a good story."

"I believe this calls for a toast," said Dr Harthill. He poured two glasses of cordial for Artie and Ham and sherry for everyone else.

"I do not normally partake of alcoholic beverages," said Constable McCorkle, accepting the drink, "but as these are exceptional circumstances, I thank you for your hospitality."

They all raised their glasses as the doctor proposed the toast. "To old soldiers everywhere, and," he added, casting a twinkling eye over the two boys, "to young adventurers too!"

"So the mystery of the Gravediggers' Club has been solved," said Ham. "Whatever shall we do next?"

"Well," replied Artie, "I daresay another mystery will present itself in due course..."

Look out for the second book of

THE
ARTIE
CONAN
DOYLE
MYSTERIES

Coming soon!

AUTHOR'S NOTE

Arthur Conan Doyle, the creator of Sherlock Holmes, was born and raised in Edinburgh, where he also studied to become a doctor. The background to his life as presented here is based on fact. The fictional aspect of the novel is the notion that young Artie experienced a series of adventures which would later inspire his famous Sherlock Holmes stories. Some of the events of *The Gravediggers' Club* are mirrored in the two great Sherlock Holmes novels *The Sign of Four* and *The Hound of the Baskervilles*. One day you should go and read them.

For more about *The Artie Conan Doyle Mysteries* and my other projects, visit my website: www.harris-authors.com

Put your
detective skills
to the test!
Are these fun facts about
Arthur Conan Doyle
TRUE or **FALSE**?

1. Arthur Conan Doyle once worked as a surgeon aboard an Arctic whaling ship.

2. The character of Sherlock Holmes was based on one of Arthur Conan Doyle's professors at medical school.

3. The first published story featuring Sherlock Holmes was called *A Study in Red*.

4. Arthur Conan Doyle was friends with the famous magician Harry Houdini.

5. Sherlock Holmes was named after Arthur Conan Doyle's family dog.

1 True 2 True, the professor's name was Joseph Bell 3 False, it was *A Study in Scarlet* 4 True 5 False

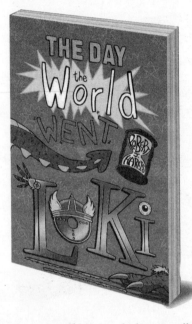

Also by Robert J. Harris

ODIN Blew Up my TV!

Book 3 in The World's Gone Loki trilogy

This time, the wise-cracking, havoc-wreaking Loki has stolen St Andrews, locked up Odin, and much more besides...

The fate of the town, and indeed the ENTIRE UNIVERSE, rests with our reluctant heroes, Lewis and Greg, and their friend Susie. Can they rescue Odin and outfox troublesome Loki before he destroys the world?

DiscoverKelpies.co.uk

Your

~~Artie Conan Doyle's~~

JOURNAL

Use these pages to solve your own mysteries!